A SINGLE THROW OF THE TARPAULIN REVEALED THE THING. The ice had melted somewhat in the heat of the room and it was clear and blue as thick, good glass. It shone wet and sleek under the harsh light of the unshielded globe above.

The room stiffened abruptly. It was face up there on the plain, greasy planks of the table. The broken half of the bronze ice-ax was still buried in the queer skull. Three mad, hate-filled eyes blazed up with a living fire, bright as fresh-spilled blood from a face ringed with a writhing, loathsome nest of worms, blue, mobile worms that crawled where hair should grow—

WHO GOES THERE?

the novella that formed the basis of THE THING

john w. campbell

 ROCKET RIDE BOOKS

Rocket Ride Books—Fiction that takes you there.
Listen to the Audio Edition of WHO GOES THERE?
www.rocketridebooks.com
inquiries@rocketridebooks.com

ISBN-13: 978-0-9823322-0-7
ISBN-10: 0-9823322-0-3

1. Title
2. Science Fiction—John W. Campbell
3. Suspense—Classic Scifi—Horror

PRINTED IN THE UNITED STATES OF AMERICA

The publisher gratefully acknowledges
the kind assistance of those
who helped make this edition possible—
**Mark Dawidziak, Barry N. Malzberg,
William F. Nolan.**

CONTENTS

"WHO GOES THERE?" was first printed in the pages of *Astounding*, in the August 1938 issue under the byline of "Don A. Stuart" (a pen name taken directly from Campbell's first wife, Dona Stuart).

By then, John W. Campbell had been writing galaxy-spanning science fiction sagas in the tradition of E.E. Smith for the better part of a decade, having achieved his first genre sale in 1930. His books would eventually include six published SF novels and a host of shorter stories covering eight collections.

In today's character-driven modern SF market most of the early Campbell fiction has become outdated, but "Who Goes There?" remains an exception. It has taken on legendary status. When it was written in the '30s, Campbell had no idea that he had created a timeless genre classic.

Its first major exposure can be credited to Raymond J. Healy and J. Francis McComas, who selected Campbell's story for book publication in their ground-breaking anthology, *Adventures in Time and Space*, from Random House in 1946. (The first anthology to use the term "Science Fiction" was *The Pocket Book of Science Fiction*, edited by Don Wollheim in 1943—which contained another classic story by "Stuart" titled "Twilight.")

The year 1951 marked a new milestone in the history of "Who Goes There?" when the story reached the big screen as *The Thing* (aka: *The Thing From Another World*). The film's producer, Howard Hawks, had optioned the motion picture rights from Campbell in the 1940s. It was a Hawks production from first frame to last, with the producer carefully monitoring director Christian Nyby. Severe plot changes were made, as the shape-changing alien is replaced by a Frankenstein-like monster. (Actor James Arness played the role, becoming famous years later as "Matt Dillon" on *Gunsmoke*.)

The Thing drew a heated response from diehard SF fans; they were not pleased with the Hawks approach. Most theater audiences, however, found it chilling and suspenseful. Critical reaction was mixed. Editor/writer Phil Hardy (in *Science Fiction: The Complete Film Scrapbook*) called it "one of the best SF movies of all time." Neil Barron, on the other hand (in *Anatomy of Wonder*), dubbed it "inept" and cited "stock horror elements."

During the same year (1951) "Who Goes There?" became the title story in a collection of Campbell's best fiction from the mid-to-late 1930s, published by Shasta Press.

All of which leads up to my personal involvement with the original story. In February of 1978, I was called into Universal Studios to create a fresh screen version of "Who Goes There?"

"We want to go back to the shape-change idea," they told me. "Get a lot closer to Campbell's original."

The screen success of my own SF novel, *Logan's Run* (MGM, 1976) had won me the Universal assignment. I re-read the story, made some notes, and arranged for a special showing of the Howard Hawks film. For me, the 1951 version did not hold up. I had remembered it as being far more subtle and effective. It now struck me as pulp melodrama, and I could see why many critics had found major problems with it.

I discarded the Hawks approach, setting out in a serious attempt to do justice to Campbell's classic. Did I pull it off? I'll let you, the reader, be the judge of that as you peruse my screen treatment following the original story.

The studio executives liked what I turned in to them in April of 1978, and I looked forward to the production. However, as is the case with so many Hollywood projects, my version was put of the shelf. "Maybe we'll do it later," they told me.

Then director John Carpenter came along with

his take on the Campbell story. Using the same 1951 title, Carpenter's version reached the screen in 1982, but was a boxoffice failure. Critic Leonard Maltin admitted that it was "more faithful to the original story," but roundly condemned its "nonstop parade of slimy, repulsive special effects that turns this into a freak show and drowns out most of the suspense."

Personally, I prefer my treatment to the Carpenter film. Yet a close friend of mine, an astute cinema buff, considers the 1982 version to be one of his favorite films.

John Wood Campbell, Jr. was born in Newark, New Jersey in 1910. He attended the Massachusetts Institute of Technology, and obtained a B.S. from Duke University in 1933. Among his early jobs, he sold cars, worked for a chemical company and as a researcher for a trucking firm. He was married twice: to Dona Stuart in 1931, and to Margaret Winter in 1950. The father of four children, he spent his off hours devouring science fiction. This led to his first writing sales in the 1930s, and as Don A. Stuart, Campbell established himself among the stellar names in the SF genre.

However, Campbell's primary impact on SF was as an editor. His influence was pivotal in the development of quality SF. In 1937 he became editor of *Astounding* (later *Analog*) and brought many of the greatest talents of this era into print, including Robert A Heinlein, A.E. van Vogt, Isaac Asimov, and Theodore Sturgeon. Campbell was tough on his writers, demanding nothing less than their best work. (He was noted for his lengthy letters full of suggestions and criticism and was rarely satisfied with the first submitted draft of any story.)

John Campbell continued to be a major editorial influence in the field until his death in the summer of 1971. The loss to SF was truly devastating.

I'm personally delighted to see "Who Goes There?" back in print in this new century. It well deserves its legendary status, and I envy the reader's thrill of discovery in encountering it for the first time in these pages.

Who goes there?

Read the story and find out!

William F. Nolan
Vancouver, WA
2009

WHO GOES THERE?
john w. campbell

THE PLACE STANK. A queer, mingled stench that only the ice-buried cabins of an Antarctic camp know, compounded of reeking human sweat, and the heavy, fish-oil stench of melted seal blubber. An overtone of liniment combated the musty smell of sweat-and-snow-drenched furs. The acrid odor of burnt cooking fat, and the animal, not-unpleasant smell of dogs, diluted by time, hung in the air.

Lingering odors of machine oil contrasted sharply with the taint of harness dressing and leather. Yet somehow, through all that reek of human beings and their associates—dogs, machines and cooking—came another taint. It was a queer, neck-ruffling thing, a faintest suggestion of an odor alien among the smells of industry and life. And it was a life-smell. But it came from the thing that lay bound with cord and tarpaulin on the table, dripping slowly, methodically onto the heavy planks, dank and gaunt under the unshielded glare of the electric light.

Blair, the little bald-pated biologist of the expedition, twitched nervously at the wrappings, exposing clear, dark ice beneath and then pulling the tarpaulin back into place restlessly. His little birdlike motions of suppressed eagerness danced his shadow across the fringe of dingy gray underwear hanging from the low ceiling, the equatorial fringe of stiff, graying hair around his naked skull a comical halo about the shadow's head.

Commander Garry brushed aside the lax legs of a suit of underwear, and stepped toward the table. Slowly his eyes traced around the rings of men sardined into the Administration Building. His tall, stiff body straightened finally, and he nodded. "Thirty-seven. All here." His voice was low, yet carried the clear authority of the commander by nature, as well as by title.

"You know the outline of the story back of that find of the Secondary Pole Expedition. I have been conferring with second-in-Command McReady, and Norris, as well as Blair and Dr. Copper. There is a difference of opinion, and because it involves the entire group, it is only just that the entire Expedition personnel act on it.

"I am going to ask McReady to give you the details of the story, because each of you has been too busy with his own work to follow closely the endeavors of the others. McReady?"

Moving from the smoke-blued background, McReady was a figure from some forgotten myth, a looming, bronze statue that held life, and walked. Six-feet-four inches he stood as he halted beside the table, and, with a characteristic glance upward to assure himself of room under the lower ceiling beam, straightened. His rough, clashingly orange windproof jacket he still had on, yet on his huge frame it did not seem misplaced. Even here, four feet beneath the drift-wind that droned across the Antarctic waste above the ceiling, the cold of the frozen continent leaked in, and gave meaning to the harshness of the man. And he was bronze—his great red-bronze beard, the heavy hair that matched it. The gnarled, corded hands gripping, relaxing, gripping and relaxing on the table planks were bronze. Even the deep-sunken eyes beneath heavy brows were bronzed.

Age-resisting endurance of the metal spoke in the cragged heavy outlines of his face, and the mellow tones of the heavy voice. "Norris and Blair agree on one thing, that animal we found was not—terrestrial in origin. Norris fears there may be danger in that; Blair says there is none.

"But I'll go back to how, and why, we found it. To all that was known before we came here, it appeared that this point was exactly over the South Magnetic Pole of Earth. The compass does point straight down here, as you all know. The more delicate instruments of the physicists, instruments especially designed for this expedition and its study of the magnetic pole, detected a secondary effect, a secondary, less powerful magnetic influence about 80 miles southwest of here.

"The Secondary Magnetic Expedition went out to investigate it. There is no need for details. We found it, but it was not the huge meteorite or magnetic mountain Norris had expected to find. Iron ore is magnetic, of course; iron more so—and certain special steels even more magnetic from the surface indications, the secondary pole we found was small, so small that the magnetic effect it had was preposterous. No magnetic material conceivable could have that effect. Soundings through the ice indicated it was within one hundred feet of the glacier surface.

"I think you should know the structure of the place. There is a broad plateau, a level sweep that runs more than 150 miles due south from the Secondary Station, Van Wall says. He didn't have time or fuel to fly farther, but it was running smoothly due south then. Right there, where that buried thing was, there is an ice-drowned mountain ridge, a granite wall of unshakable strength that has damned back the ice creeping from the south.

"And four hundred miles due south is the South Polar Plateau. You have asked me at various times why it gets warmer here when the wind rises, and most of you know. As a meteorologist I'd have staked my word that no wind could blow at –70 degrees;

that no more than a 5-mile wind could blow at –50; without causing warming due to friction with ground, snow and ice and the air itself.

"We camped there on the lip of that ice-drowned mountain range for twelve days. We dug out camp into the blue ice that formed the surface, and escaped most of it. But for twelve consecutive days the wind blew at 45 miles an hour. It went as high as 48, and fell to 41 at times. The temperature was –63 degrees. It rose to –60 and fell to –68. It was meteorologically impossible, and it went on uninterruptedly for twelve days and twelve nights.

"Somewhere to the south, the frozen air of the South Polar Plateau slides down from that 18,000-foot bowl, down a mountain pass, over a glacier, and starts north. There must be a funneling mountain chain that directs it, and sweeps it away for four hundred miles to hit that bald plateau where we found the secondary pole, and 350 miles farther north reaches the Antarctic Ocean.

"It's been frozen there since Antarctica froze twenty million years ago. There never has been a thaw there.

"Twenty million years ago Antarctica was beginning to freeze. We've investigated, thought and built speculations. What we believe happened was about like this.

"Something came down out of space, a ship. We saw it there in the blue ice, a thing like a submarine without a conning tower or directive vanes, 280 feet long and 45 feet in diameter at its thickest.

"Eh, Van Wall? Space? Yes, but I'll explain that better later." McReady's steady voice went on.

"It came down from space, driven and lifted by forces men haven't discovered yet, and somehow—perhaps something went wrong then—it tangled with Earth's magnetic field. It came south here, out of control probably, circling the magnetic pole. That's a savage country there, but when Antarctica was still freezing it must have been a thousand times more savage. There must have been blizzard snow, as well as drift, new snow falling as the continent glaciated. The swirl there must have been particularly bad, the wind hurling a solid blanket of white over the lip of that now-buried mountain.

"The ship struck solid granite head-on, and cracked up. Not every one of the passengers in it was killed, but the ship must have been ruined, her driving mechanism locked. It tangled with Earth's field, Norris believes. No thing made by intelligent beings can tangle with the dead immensity of a planet's natural forces and survive.

"One of its passengers stepped out. The wind we saw there never fell below 41, and the temperature never rose above –60. Then—the wind must have been stronger. And there was drift falling in a solid sheet. The thing was lost completely in ten paces."

He paused for a moment, the deep, steady voice giving way to the drone of wind overhead, and the uneasy, malicious gurgling in the pipe of the galley stove.

Drift—a drift-wind was sweeping by overhead.

Right now the snow picked up by the mumbling wind fled in level, blinding lines across the face of the buried camp. If a man stepped out of the tunnels that connected each of the camp buildings beneath the surface, he'd be lost in ten paces. Out there, the slim, black finger of the radio mast lifted three hundred feet into the air, and at its peak was the clear night sky. A sky of thin, whining wind rushing steadily from beyond to another beyond under the licking, curling mantle of the aurora. And off north, the horizon flamed with queer, angry colors of the midnight twilight. That was Spring three hundred feet above Antarctica.

At the surface—it was white death. Death of a needle-fingered cold driven before the wind, sucking heat from any warm thing. Cold—and white mist of endless, everlasting drift, the fine, fine particles of licking snow that obscured all things.

Kinner, the little, scar-faced cook, winced. Five days ago he had stepped out to the surface to reach a cache of frozen beef. He had reached it, started back—and the drift-wind leapt out of the south. Cold, white death that streamed across the ground blinded him in twenty seconds. He stumbled on wildly in circles. It was half an hour before rope-guided men from below found him in the impenetrable murk.

It was easy for man—or *thing*—to get lost in ten paces.

"And the drift-wind then was probably more impenetrable than we know." McReady's voice snapped Kinner's mind back. Back to the welcome,

dank warmth of the Ad Building. "The passenger of
the ship wasn't prepared either, it appears. It froze
within ten feet of the ship.

"We dug down to find the ship, and our tunnel
happened to find the frozen—animal. Barclay's ice-
ax struck its skull.

"When we saw what it was, Barclay went back to
the tractor, started the fire up and when the steam
pressure built, sent a call for Blair and Dr. Copper.
Barclay himself was sick then. Stayed sick for three
days, as a matter of fact.

"When Blair and Copper came, we cut out the
animal in a block of ice, as you see, wrapped it and
loaded it on the tractor for return here. We wanted
to get into that ship.

"We reached the side and found the metal was
something we didn't know. Our beryllium-bronze,
non-magnetic tools wouldn't touch it. Barclay had
some tool-steel on the tractor, and that wouldn't
scratch it either. We made reasonable tests—even
tried some acid from the batteries with no results.

"They must have had a passivating process to
make magnesium metal resist acid that way, and
the alloy must have been at least ninety-five per cent
magnesium. But we had no way of guessing that, so
when we spotted the barely opened locked door, we
cut around it. There was clear, hard ice inside the
lock, where we couldn't reach it. Through the little
crack we could look in and see that only metal and
tools were in there, so we decided to loosen the ice
with a bomb.

"We had decanite bombs and thermite. Thermite is the ice-softener; decanite might have shattered valuable things, where the thermite's heat would just loosen the ice. Dr. Copper, Norris and I placed a twenty-five-pound thermite bomb, wired it, and took the connector up the tunnel to the surface, where Blair had the steam tractor waiting. A hundred yards the other side of that granite wall we set off the thermite bomb.

"The magnesium metal of the ship caught, of course. The glow of the bomb flared and died, then it began to flare again. We ran back to the tractor, and gradually the glare built up. From where we were we could see the whole ice-field illuminated from beneath with an unbearable light; the ship's shadow was a great, dark cone reaching off toward the north, where the twilight was just about gone. For a moment it lasted, and we counted three other shadow-things that might have been other—passengers—frozen there. Then the ice was crashing down and against the ship.

"That's why I told you about that place. The wind sweeping down from the Pole was at our backs. Steam and hydrogen flame were torn away in white ice-fog; the flaming heat under the ice there was yanked away toward the Antarctic Ocean before it touched us. Otherwise we wouldn't have come back, even with the shelter of that granite ridge that stopped the light.

"Somehow in the blinding inferno we could see great hunched things, black bulks glowing, even so.

They shed even the furious incandescence of the magnesium for a time. Those must have been the engines, we knew. Secrets going in blazing glory— secrets that might have given Man the planets. Mysterious things that could lift and hurl that ship—and had soaked in the force of the Earth's magnetic field. I saw Norris' mouth move, and ducked. I couldn't hear him.

"Insulation—something—gave way. All Earth's field they'd soaked up twenty million years before broke loose. The aurora in the sky above licked down, and the whole plateau there was bathed in cold fire that blanketed vision. The ice-ax in my hand got red hot, and hissed on the ice. Metal buttons on my clothes burned into me. And a flash of electric blue seared upward from beyond the granite wall.

"Then the walls of ice crashed down on it. For an instant it squealed the way dry-ice does when it's pressed between metal.

"We were blind and groping in the dark for hours while our eyes recovered. We found every coil within a mile was fused rubbish, the dynamo and every radio set, the earphones and speakers. If we hadn't had the steam tractor, we wouldn't have gotten over to the Secondary Camp.

"Van Wall flew in from Big Magnet at sun-up, as you know. We came home as soon as possible. That is the history of—that." McReady's great bronze beard gestured toward the thing on the table.

TWO

BLAIR STIRRED UNEASILY, his little bony fingers wriggling under the harsh light. Little brown freckles on his knuckles slid back and forth as the tendons under the skin twitched. He pulled aside a bit of the tarpaulin and looked impatiently at the dark icebound thing inside.

McReady's big body straightened somewhat. He'd ridden the rocking, jarring steam tractor forty miles that day, pushing on to Big Magnet here. Even his calm will had been pressed by the anxiety to mix again with humans. It was lone and quiet out there in Secondary Camp, where a wolf-wind howled down from the Pole. Wolf-wind howling in his sleep—winds droning and the evil, unspeakable face of that monster leering up as he'd first seen it through clear, blue ice, with a bronze ice-ax buried in its skull.

The giant meteorologist spoke again. "The problem is them. Blair wants to examine the thing. Thaw it out and make micro slides of its tissues and so forth. Norris doesn't believe that is safe, and Blair does. Dr. Copper agrees pretty much with Blair. Norris is a physicist, of course, not a biologist. But he makes a point I think we should all hear. Blair has described the microscopic life-forms biologists find living, even in this cold an inhospitable place. They freeze every winter, and thaw every summer—for three months—and live.

"The point Norris makes is—they thaw, and live again. There must have been microscopic life associated with this creature. There is with every living thing we know. And Norris is afraid that we may release a plague—some germ disease unknown to Earth—if we thaw those microscopic things that have been frozen there for twenty million years.

"Blair admits that such micro-life might retain the power of living. Such unorganized things as individual cells can retain life for unknown periods, when solidly frozen. The beast itself is as dead as those frozen mammoths they find in Siberia. Organized, highly developed life-forms can't stand that treatment.

"But micro-life could. Norris suggests that we may release some disease-form that man, never having met it before, will be utterly defenseless against.

"Blair's answer is that there may be such still-living

germs, but that Norris has the case reversed. They are utterly non-immune to man. Our life chemistry probably—"

"Probably!" The little biologist's head lifted in a quick, birdlike motion. The halo of gray hair about his bald head ruffled as though angry. "Heh. One look—"

"I know," McReady acknowledged. "The thing is not Earthly. It does not seem likely that it can have a life-chemistry sufficiently like ours to make cross-infection remotely possible. I would say that there is no danger."

McReady looked toward Dr. Copper. The physician shook his head slowly. "None whatever," he asserted confidently. "Man cannot infect or be infected by germs that live in such comparatively close relatives as the snakes. And they are, I assure you," his clean-shaven face grimaced uneasily, "*much* nearer to us than—*that*."

Vance Norris moved angrily. He was comparatively short in this gathering of big men, some five-feet-eight, and his stocky, powerful build tended to make him seem shorter. His black hair was crisp and hard, like short, steel wires, and his eyes were the gray of fractured steel. If McReady was a man of bronze, Norris was all steel. His movements, his thoughts, his whole bearing had the quick, hard impulse of steel spring. His nerves were steel—hard, quick-acting—swift corroding.

He was decided on his point now, and he lashed out in its defense with a characteristic quick, clipped flow of words. "Different chemistry be damned. That thing may be dead—or, by God, it may not—but I don't like it. Damn it, Blair, let them see the monstrosity you are petting over there. Let them see the foul thing and decide for themselves whether they want that thing thawed out in this camp.

"Thawed out, by the way. That's got to be thawed out in one of the shacks tonight, if it is thawed out. Somebody—who's watchman tonight? Magnetic—oh, Connant. Cosmic rays tonight. Well, you get to sit up with that twenty-million-year-old mummy of his.

"Unwrap it, Blair. How the hell can they tell what they are buying if they can't see it? It may have a different chemistry. I don't know what else it has, but I know it has something I don't want. If you can judge by the look on its face—it isn't human so maybe you can't—it was annoyed when it froze. Annoyed, in fact, is just about as close an approximation of the way it felt as crazy, mad, insane hatred. Neither one touches the subject.

"How the hell can these birds tell what they are voting on? They haven't seen those three red eyes, and the blue hair like crawling worms. Crawling—damn, it's crawling there in the ice right now!

"Nothing Earth ever spawned had the unutterable sublimation of devastating wrath that thing let loose in its face when it looked around this frozen desolation twenty million years ago. Mad? It was mad clear through—searing, blistering mad!

"Hell, I've had bad dreams ever since I looked at

those three red eyes. Nightmares. Dreaming the thing thawed out and came to life—that it wasn't dead, or even wholly unconscious all those twenty million years, but just slowed, waiting—waiting. You'll dream, too, while that damned thing that Earth wouldn't own is dripping, dripping in the Cosmos House tonight.

"And, Connant," Norris whipped toward the cosmic ray specialist, "won't you have fun sitting up all night in the quiet. Wind whining above—and that thing dripping—" He stopped for a moment, and looked around.

"I know. That's not science. But this is, it's psychology. You'll have nightmares for a year to come. Every night since I looked at that thing I've had 'em. That's why I hate it—sure I do—and don't want it around. Put it back where it came from and let it freeze for another twenty million years. I had some swell nightmares—that it wasn't made like we are—which is obvious—but of a different kind of flesh that it can really control. That it can change its shape, and look like a man—and wait to kill and eat—

"That's not a logical argument. I know it isn't. The thing isn't Earth-logic anyway.

"Maybe it has an alien body-chemistry, and maybe its bugs do have a different body-chemistry. A germ might not stand that, but, Blair and Copper, how about a virus? That's just an enzyme molecule, you've said. That wouldn't need anything but a protein molecule of any body to work on.

"And how are you so sure that, of the million of varieties of microscopic life it may have, none of them are dangerous? How about diseases like hydrophobia—rabies—that attacks any warm-blooded creature, whatever its body-chemistry may be? And parrot fever? Have you a body like a parrot, Blair? And plain rot—gangrene—necrosis, do you want? That isn't choosy about body-chemistry!"

Blair looked up from his puttering long enough to meet Norris' angry gray eyes for an instant. "So far the only thing you have said this thing gave off that was catching was dreams. I'll go so far as to admit that." An impish, slightly malignant grin crossed the little man's seamed face. "I had some, too. So. It's dream-infectious. No doubt an exceedingly dangerous malady.

"So far as your other things go, you have a badly mistaken idea about viruses. In the first place, nobody has shown that the enzyme-molecule theory, and that alone, explains them. And in the second place, when you catch tobacco mosaic or wheat rust, let me know. A wheat plant is a lot nearer your body-chemistry than this other-world creature is.

"And your rabies is limited, strictly limited. You can't get it from, nor give it to, a wheat plant or a fish—which is a collateral descendant of a common ancestor of yours. Which this, Norris, is not." Blair nodded pleasantly toward the tarpaulined bulk on the table.

"Well, thaw the damned thing in a tub of formalin if you must thaw it. I've suggested that—"

"And I've said there would be no sense in it. You can't compromise. Why did you and Commander Garry come down here to study magnetism? Why weren't you content to stay at home? There's magnetic force enough in New York. I could no more study the life this thing once had from a formalin-pickled sample than you could get the information you wanted back in New York. And—if this one is so treated, *never in all time to come can there be a duplicate*! The race it came from must have passed away in the twenty millions years it lay frozen, so that even if it came from Mars then, we'd never find its like. And—the ship is gone.

"There's only one way to do this—and that is the best possible way. It must be thawed slowly, carefully, and not in formalin."

Commander Garry stood forward again, and Norris stepped back muttering angrily. "I think Blair is right, gentlemen. What do you say?"

Connant grunted. "It sounds right to us, I think—only perhaps he ought to stand watch over it while it's thawing." He grinned ruefully, brushing a stray lock of ripe-cherry hair back from his forehead. "Swell idea, in fact—if he sits up with his jolly little corpse."

Garry smiled slightly. A general chuckle of agreement rippled over the group. "I should think any ghost it may have had would have starved to death if it hung around here that long, Connant," Garry suggested. "And you look capable of taking care of it. 'Ironman' Connant ought to be able to take out any opposing players, still."

Connant shook himself uneasily. "I'm not worrying about ghosts. Let's see that thing. I—"

Eagerly Blair was stripping back the ropes. A single throw of the tarpaulin revealed the thing. The ice had melted somewhat in the heat of the room and it was clear and blue as thick, good glass. It shone wet and sleek under the harsh light of the unshielded globe above.

The room stiffened abruptly. It was face up there on the plain, greasy planks of the table. The broken half of the bronze ice-ax was still buried in the queer skull. Three mad, hate-filled eyes blazed up with a living fire, bright as fresh-spilled blood from a face ringed with a writhing, loathsome nest of worms, blue, mobile worms that crawled where hair should grow—

Van Wall, six feet and two hundred pounds of ice-nerved pilot, gave a queer, strangled gasp and butted, stumbled his way out to the corridor. Half the company broke for the doors. The others stumbled away from the table.

McReady stood at one end of the table watching them, his great body planted solid on his powerful legs. Norris from the opposite end glowered at the thing with smoldering heat. Outside the door, Garry was talking with half a dozen of the men at once.

Blair had a tack hammer. The ice that cased the thing *schluffed* crisply under its steel claw as it peeled from the thing it had cased for twenty thousand thousand years—

THREE

I KNOW YOU DON'T LIKE that thing, Connant, but it just has to be thawed out right. You say leave it as it is till we get back to civilization. All right, I'll admit your argument that we could do a better and more complete job there is sound. But—how are we going to get this across the Line? We have to take this through one temperate zone, the equatorial zone, and half way through the other temperate zone before we get it to New York. You don't want to sit with it one night, but you suggest, then, that I hang its corpse in the freezer with the beef?" Blair looked up from his cautious chipping, his bald, freckled skull nodding triumphantly.

Kinner, the stocky, scar-faced cook, saved Connant

the trouble of answering. "Hey, you listen, mister. You put that thing in the box with the meat, and by all the gods there ever were, I'll put you in to keep it company. You birds have brought everything movable in this camp in onto my mess tables here already, and I had to stand for that. But you go putting things like that in my meat box or even my meat cache here, and you cook your own damn grub."

"But, Kinner, this is the only table in Big Magnet that's big enough to work on," Blair objected. "Everybody's explained that."

"Yeah, and everybody's brought everything in here. Clark brings his dogs every time there's a fight and sews them up on that table. Ralsen brings in his sledges. Hell, the only thing you haven't had on that table is the Boeing. And youda had that in if you coulda figured a way to get it through the tunnels."

Commander Garry chuckled and grinned at Van Wall, the huge Chief Pilot. Van Wall's great blond beard twitched suspiciously as he nodded gravely to Kinner. "You're right, Kinner. The aviation department is the only one that treats you right."

"It does get crowded, Kinner," Garry acknowledged. "But I'm afraid we all find it that way at times. Not much privacy in an Antarctic camp."

"Privacy? What the hell's that? You know, the thing that really made me weep, was when I saw Barclay marchin' through here chantin' 'The last lumber in the camp! The last lumber in the camp!' and carryin' it out to build that house on his tractor. Damn it,

I missed that moon cut in the door he carried out more'n I missed the sun when it set. That wasn't just the last lumber Barclay was walkin' off with. He was carryin' off the last bit of privacy in this blasted place."

A grin rode even on Connant's heavy face as Kinner's perennial good-natured grouch came up again. But it died away quickly as his dark, deep-set eyes turned again to the red-eyed thing Blair was chipping from its cocoon of ice. A big hand ruffed his shoulder-length hair, and tugged at a twisted lock that fell behind his ear in a familiar gesture. "I know that cosmic ray shack's going to be too crowded if I have to sit up with that thing," he growled. "Why can't you go on chipping the ice away from around it—you can do that without anybody butting in, I assure you—and then hang the thing up over the power-plant boiler? That's warm enough. It'll thaw out a chicken, even a whole side of beef, in a few hours."

"I know." Blair protested, dropping the tack hammer to gesture more effectively with his bony, freckled fingers, his small body tense with eagerness, "but this is too important to take any chances. There never was a find like this; there never can be again. It's the only chance men will ever have, and it has to be done exactly right.

"Look, you know how the fish we caught down near the Ross Sea would freeze almost as soon as we got them on deck, and come to life again if we thawed them gently? Low forms of life aren't killed by quick freezing and slow thawing. We have—"

"Hey, for the love of Heaven—you mean that damned thing will come to life!" Connant yelled. "You get the damned thing—Let me at it! That's going to be in so many pieces—"

"No! *No*, you fool—" Blair jumped in front of Connant to protect his precious find. "No. Just *low* forms of life. For Pete's sake let me finish. You can't thaw higher forms of life and have them come to. Wait a moment now—hold it! A fish can come to after freezing because it's so low a form of life that the individual cells of its body can revive, and that alone is enough to reestablish life. Any higher forms thawed out that way are dead. Though the individual cells revive, they die because there must be organization and cooperative effort to live. That cooperation cannot be reestablished. There is a sort of potential life in any uninjured, quick-frozen animal. But it can't—can't under any circumstances—become active life in higher animals. The higher animals are too complex, too delicate. This is an intelligent creature as high in its evolution as we are in ours. Perhaps higher. It is as dead as a frozen man would be."

"How do you know?" demanded Connant, hefting the ice-ax he had seized a moment before.

Commander Garry laid a restraining hand on his heavy shoulder. "Wait a minute, Connant. I want to get this straight. I agree that there is going to be no thawing of this thing if there is the remotest chance of its revival. I quite agree it is much too unpleasant to have alive, but I had no idea there was the remotest possibility."

Dr. Copper pulled his pipe from between his teeth and heaved his stocky, dark body from the bunk he had been sitting in. "Blair's being technical. That's dead. As dead as the mammoths they find frozen in Siberia. Potential life is like atomic energy—there, but nobody can get it out, and it certainly won't release itself except in rare cases, as rare as radium in the chemical analogy. We have all sorts of proof that things don't live after being frozen—not even fish, generally speaking—and no proof that higher animal life can under any circumstances. What's the point, Blair?"

The little biologist shook himself. The little ruff of hair standing out around his bald pate waved in righteous anger. "The point is," he said in an injured tone, "that the individual cells might show the characteristics they had in life, if it is properly thawed. A man's muscle cells live many hours after he has died. Just because they live, and a few things like hair and fingernail cells still live, you wouldn't accuse a corpse of being a zombie, or something.

"Now if I thaw this right, I may have a chance to determine what sort of world it's native to. We don't, and can't know by any other means, whether it came from Earth or Mars or Venus or from beyond the stars.

"And just because it looks unlike men, you don't have to accuse it of being evil, or vicious or something. Maybe that expression on its face is its equivalent to a resignation to fate. White is the color of mourning to the Chinese. If men can have different customs, why can't a so-different race have different understandings of facial expressions?"

Connant laughed softly, mirthlessly. "Peaceful resignation! If that is the best it could do in the way of resignation, I should exceedingly dislike seeing it when it was looking mad. That face was never designed to express peace. It just didn't have any philosophical thoughts like peace in its make-up.

"I know it's your pet—but be sane about it. The thing grew up on evil, adolesced slowly roasting alive the local equivalent of kittens, and amused itself through maturity on new and ingenious torture."

"You haven't the slightest right to say that," snapped Blair. "How do you know the first thing about the meaning of a facial expression inherently inhuman! It may well have no human equivalent whatever. That is just a different development of Nature, another example of Nature's wonderful adaptability. Growing on another, perhaps harsher world, it has different form and features. But it is just as much a legitimate child of Nature as you are. You are displaying the childish human weakness of hating the different. On its own world it would probably class you as a fish-belly, white monstrosity with an insufficient number of eyes and a fungoid body pale and bloated with gas.

"Just because its nature is different, you haven't any right to say it's necessarily evil."

Norris burst out a single, explosive, "Haw!" He

looked down at the thing. "May be that things from other worlds don't *have* to be evil just because they're different. But that thing *was*! Child of Nature, eh? Well, it was a hell of an evil Nature."

"Aw, will you mugs cut crabbing at each other and get the damned thing off my table?" Kinner growled. "And put a canvas over it. It looks indecent."

"Kinner's gone modest," jeered Connant.

Kinner slanted his eyes up to the big physicist. The scarred cheek twisted to join the line of his tight lips in a twisted grin. "All right, big boy, and what were you grousing about a minute ago? We can set the thing in a chair next to you tonight, if you want."

"I'm not afraid of its face," Connant snapped. "I don't like keeping awake over its corpse particularly, but I'm going to do it."

Kinner's grin spread. "Uh-huh." He went off to the galley stove and shook down ashes vigorously, drowning the brittle chipping of the ice as Blair fell to work again.

FOUR

"CLUCK," reported the cosmic ray counter, "*cluck-burrrp-cluck.*" Connant started and dropped his pencil.

"Damnation." The physicist looked toward the far corner, back at the Geiger counter on the table near that corner, and crawled under the desk at which he had been working to retrieve the pencil. He sat down at his work again, trying to make his writing more even. It tended to have jerks and quavers in it, in time with the abrupt proud-hen noises of the Geiger counter. The muted whoosh of the pressure lamp he was using for illumination, the mingled gargles and bugle calls of a dozen men sleeping down the corridor in Paradise House formed the background sounds for the irregular, clucking noises of the counter, the occasional rustle of falling coal in the copper-bellied stove. And a soft, steady *drip-drip-drip* from the thing in the corner.

Connant jerked a pack of cigarettes from his pocket, snapped it so that a cigarette protruded and jabbed the cylinder into his mouth. The lighter failed to function, and he pawed angrily through the pile of papers in search of a match. He scratched the wheel of the lighter several times, dropped it with a curse and got up to pluck a hot coal from the stove with the coal tongs.

The lighter functioned instantly when he tried it on returning to the desk. The counter ripped out a series of chucking guffaws as a burst of cosmic rays struck through to it. Connant turned to glower at it, and tried to concentrate on the interpretation of data collected during the past week. The weekly summary—

He gave up and yielded to curiosity, or nervousness. He lifted the pressure lamp from the desk and carried it over to the table in the corner. Then he returned to the stove and picked up the coal tongs. The beast had been thawing for nearly eighteen hours now. He poked at it with an unconscious caution; the flesh was no longer hard as armor plate, but had assumed a rubbery texture. It looked like wet, blue rubber glistening under droplets of water like little round jewels in the glare of the gasoline pressure lantern. Connant felt an unreasoning desire to pour the contents of the lamp's reservoir over the thing in its box and drop the cigarette into it. The three red eyes glared up at him sightlessly, the ruby eyeballs reflecting murky, smoky rays of light.

He realized vaguely that he had been looking at them for a very long time, even vaguely understood that they were no longer sightless. But it did not seem of importance, of no more importance than the labored, slow motion of the tentacular things that sprouted from the base of the scrawny, slowly pulsing neck.

Connant picked up the pressure lamp and returned to his chair. He sat down, staring at the pages of mathematics before him. The clucking of the counter was strangely less disturbing, the rustle of the coals in the stove no longer distracting.

The creak of the floorboards behind him didn't interrupt his thoughts as he went about his weekly report in an automatic manner, filling in columns of data and making brief, summarizing notes.

The creak of the floorboard sounded nearer.

FIVE

BLAIR CAME UP from the nightmare-haunted depths of sleep abruptly. Connant's face floated vaguely above him; for a moment it seemed a continuance of the wild horror of the dream. But Connant's face was angry, and a little frightened. "Blair—Blair you damned log, wake up."

"Uh-eh?" the little biologist rubbed his eyes, his bony, freckled fingers crooked to a mutilated child-fist. From surrounding bunks other faces lifted to stare down at them.

Connant straightened up. "Get up—and get a lift on. Your damned animal's escaped."

"Escaped—what!" Chief Pilot Van Walls's bull voice roared out with a volume that shook the walls. Down the communication tunnels other voices yelled suddenly. The dozen inhabitants of Paradise House tumbled in abruptly, Barclay, stocky and bulbous in long woolen underwear, carrying a fire extinguisher.

"What the hell's the matter?" Barclay demanded.

"Your damned beast got loose. I fell asleep about twenty minutes ago, and when I woke up, the thing was gone. Hey, Doc, the hell you say those things can't come to life. Blair's blasted potential life developed a hell of a lot of potential and walked out on us."

Copper stared blankly. "It wasn't—Earthly," he sighed suddenly. "I—I guess Earthly laws don't apply."

"Well, it applied for leave of absence and took it. We've got to find it and capture it somehow." Connant swore bitterly, his deep-set black eyes sullen and angry. "It's a wonder the hellish creature didn't eat me in my sleep."

Blair stared back, his pale eyes suddenly fearstruck. "Maybe it di—er—uh—we'll have to find it."

"You find it. It's your pet. I've had all I want to do with it, sitting there for seven hours with the counter clucking every few seconds, and you birds in here singing night-music. It's a wonder I got to sleep. I'm going through to the Ad Building."

Commander Garry ducked through the doorway, pulling his belt tight. "You won't have to. Van's roar sounded like the Boeing taking off down wind. So it wasn't dead?"

"I didn't carry it off in my arms, I assure you,"

Connant snapped. "The last I saw, that split skull was oozing green goo, like a squashed caterpillar. Doc just said our laws don't work—it's unearthly. Well, it's an unearthly monster, with an unearthly disposition, judging by the face, wandering around with a split skull and brains oozing out."

Norris and McReady appeared in the doorway, a doorway filling with other shivering men. "Has anybody seen it coming over here?" Norris asked innocently. "About four feet tall—three red eyes—brains oozing—Hey, has anybody checked to make sure this isn't a cracked idea of humor? If it is, I think we'll unite in tying Blair's pet around Connant's neck like the ancient Mariner's albatross."

"It's no humor," Connant shivered. "Lord, I wish it were. I'd rather wear—" He stopped. A wild, weird howl shrieked through the corridors. The men stiffened abruptly, and half turned.

"I think it's been located," Connant finished. His dark eyes shifted with a queer unease. He darted back to his bunk in Paradise house, to return almost immediately with a heavy .45 revolver and an ice-ax. He hefted both gently as he started for the corridor toward Dogtown. "It blundered down the wrong corridor—and landed among the huskies. Listen—the dogs have broken their chains—"

The half-terrorized howl of the dog pack changed to a wild hunting melee. The voices of the dogs thundered in the narrow corridors, and through them came a low rippling snarl of distilled hate. A shrill of pain, a dozen snarling yelps.

Connant broke for the door. Close behind him, McReady, then Barclay and Commander Garry came. Other men broke for the Ad Building, and weapons—the sledge house. Pomroy, in charge of Big Magnet's five cows, started down the corridor in the opposite direction—he had a six-foot-handled, long-tined pitchfork in mind.

Barclay slid to a halt, as McReady's giant bulk turned abruptly away from the tunnel leading to Dogtown, and vanished off at an angle. Uncertainly, the mechanician wavered a moment, the fire extinguisher in his hands, hesitating from one side to the other. Then he was racing after Connant's broad back. Whatever McReady had in mind, he could be trusted to make it work.

Connant stopped at the bend in the corridor. His breath hissed suddenly through his throat. "Great God—" The revolver exploded thunderously; three numbing, palpable waves of sound crashed through the confined corridors. Two more. The revolver dropped to the hard-packed snow of the trail, and Barclay saw the ice-ax shift into defensive position. Connant's powerful body blocked his vision, but beyond he heard something mewing, and, insanely, chuckling. The dogs were quieter; there was a deadly seriousness in their low snarls. Taloned feet scratched at hard-packed snow, broken chains were clinking and tangling.

Connant shifted abruptly, and Barclay could see what lay beyond. For a second he stood frozen, then his breath went out in a gusty curse. The Thing launched itself at Connant, the powerful arms of the man swung the ice-ax flatside first at what might have been a hand. It scrunched horribly, and the tattered flesh, ripped by a half-dozen savage huskies, leapt to its feet again. The red eyes blazed with an unearthly hatred, an unearthly, unkillable vitality.

Barclay turned the fire extinguisher on it; the blinding, blistering stream of chemical spray confused it, baffled it, together with the savage attacks of the huskies, not for long afraid of anything that did, or could live, held it at bay.

McReady wedged men out of his way and drove down the narrow corridor packed with men unable to reach the scene. There was a sure fore-planned drive to McReady's attack. One of the giant blowtorches used in warming the plane's engines was in his bronzed hands. It roared gustily as he turned the corner and opened the valve. The mad mewing hissed louder. The dogs scrambled back from the three-foot lance of blue-hot flame.

"Bar, get a power cable, run it in somehow. And a handle. We can electrocute this—monster, if I don't incinerate it." McReady spoke with an authority of planned action. Barclay turned down the long corridor to the power plant, but already before him Norris and Van Wall were racing down.

Barclay found the cable in the electrical cache in the tunnel wall. In a half minute he was hacking at it, walking back. Van Wall's voice rang out in a warning shout of "Power!" as the emergency gasoline-powered dynamo thudded into action. Half a dozen other men were down there now; the coal, kindling were going into the firebox of the steam power plant. Norris, cursing in a low, deadly monotone, was working with quick, sure fingers on the other end of Barclay's cable, splicing in a contactor in one of the power leads.

The dogs had fallen back when Barclay reached the corridor bend, fallen back before a furious monstrosity that glared from baleful red eyes, mewing in trapped hatred. The dogs were a semi-circle of red-dipped muzzles with a fringe of glistening white teeth, whining with a vicious eagerness that near matched the fury of the red eyes. McReady stood confidently alert at the corridor bend, the gustily muttering torch held loose and ready for action in his hands. He stepped aside without moving his eyes from the beast as Barclay came up. There was a slight, tight smile on his lean, bronzed face.

Norris' voice called down the corridor, and Barclay stepped forward. The cable was taped to the long handle of a snow-shovel, the two conductors split, and held eighteen inches apart by a scrap of lumber lashed at right angles across the far end of the handle. Bare copper conductors, charged with 220 volts, glinted in the light of pressure lamps. The Thing mewed and hated and dodged. McReady advanced to Barclay's side. The dogs beyond sensed the plan with the almost-telepathic intelligence of trained huskies. Their whimpering grew shriller, softer, their mincing steps carried them nearer. Abruptly a huge, night-black Alaskan leapt onto the trapped thing. It turned squalling, saber-clawed feet slashing.

Barclay leapt forward and jabbed. A weird, shrill scream rose and choked out. The smell of burnt flesh in the corridor intensified; greasy smoke curled up. The echoing pound of the gas-electric dynamo down the corridor became a slogging thud.

The red eyes clouded over in a stiffening, jerking travesty of a face. Armlike, leglike members quivered and jerked. The dogs leapt forward, and Barclay yanked back his shovel-handled weapon. The thing on the snow did not move as gleaming teeth ripped it open.

SIX

GARRY LOOKED ABOUT the crowded room. Thirty-two men, some tensed nervously standing against the wall, some uneasily relaxed, some sitting, most perforce standing, as intimate as sardines. Thirty-two, plus the five engaged in sewing up wounded dogs, made thirty-seven, the total personnel.

Garry started speaking. "All right, I guess we're here. Some of you—three or four at most—saw what happened. All of you have seen that thing on the table, and can get a general idea. Anyone hasn't, I'll lift—" His hand strayed to the tarpaulin bulking over the thing on the table. There was an acrid odor of singed flesh seeping out of it. The men, stirred restlessly, hasty denials.

"It looks rather as though Charnauk isn't going to lead any more teams," Garry went on. "Blair wants to get at this thing, and make some more detailed examination. We want to know what happened, and make sure right now that this is permanently, totally dead. Right?"

Connant grinned. "Anybody that doesn't agree can sit up with it tonight."

"All right then, Blair, what can you say about it? What was it?" Garry turned to the little biologist.

"I wonder if we ever saw its natural form," Blair looked at the covered mass. "It may have been imitating the beings that built that ship—but I don't think it was. I think that was its true form. Those of us who were up near the bend saw the thing in action; the thing on the table is the result. When it got loose, apparently, it started looking around. Antarctica still frozen as it was ages ago when the creature first saw it—and froze. From my observations while it was thawing out, and the bits of tissue I cut and hardened then, I think it was native to a hotter planet than Earth. It couldn't, in its natural form, stand the temperature. There is no life-form on Earth that can live in Antarctica during the winter, but the best compromise is the dog. It found the dogs, and somehow got near enough to Charnauk to get him. The others smelled it—heard it—I don't know—anyway they went wild, and broke chains, and attacked it before it was finished. The thing we found was part Charnauk, queerly only half-dead, part Charnauk half-digested by the jellylike protoplasm of that creature, and part the remains of the thing we originally found, sort of melted down to the basic protoplasm.

"When the dogs attacked it, it turned into the best fighting thing it could think of. Some other-world beast apparently."

"Turned," snapped Garry. "How?"

"Every living thing is made up of jelly—protoplasm and minute, submicroscopic things called nuclei, which control the bulk, the protoplasm. This thing was just a modification of that same worldwide plan of Nature; cells made up of protoplasm, controlled by infinitely tinier nuclei. You physicists might compare it—an individual cell of any living thing—with an atom; the bulk of the atom, the space-filling part, is made up of the electron orbits, but the character of the thing is determined by the atomic nucleus.

"This isn't wildly beyond what we already know. It's just a modification we haven't seen before. It's as natural, as logical, as any other manifestation of life. It obeys exactly the same laws. The cells are made of protoplasm, their character determined by the nucleus.

"Only in this creature, the cell-nuclei can control those cells at *will*. It digested Charnauk, and as it digested, studied every cell of his tissue, and shaped its own cells to imitate them exactly. Parts of it— parts that had time to finish changing—are dog-cells. But they don't have dog-cell nuclei." Blair lifted a fraction of the tarpaulin. A torn dog's leg with stiff gray fur protruded. "That, for instance, isn't dog at all; it's imitation. Some parts I'm certain about; the nucleus was hiding itself, covering up with dog-cell imitation nucleus. In time, not even a microscope would have shown the difference."

"Suppose," asked Norris bitterly, "it had had lots of time?"

"Then it would have been a dog. The other dogs would have accepted it. We would have accepted it. I don't think anything would have distinguished it, not microscope, nor X-ray, nor any other means. This is a member of a supremely intelligent race, a race that has learned the deepest secrets of biology, and turned them to its use."

"What was it planning to do?" Barclay looked at the humped tarpaulin.

Blair grinned unpleasantly. The wavering halo of thin hair round his bald pate wavered in the stir of air. "Take over the world, I imagine."

"Take over the world! Just it, all by itself?" Connant gasped. "Set itself up as a lone dictator?"

"No," Blair shook his head. The scalpel he had been fumbling in his bony fingers dropped; he bent to pick it up, so that his face was hidden as he spoke. "It would become the population of the world."

"Become—populate the world? Does it reproduce asexually?"

Blair shook his head and gulped. "It's—it doesn't have to. It weighed eighty-five pounds. Charnauk weighed about ninety. It would have become Charnauk, and had eighty-five pounds left, to become—oh, Jack for instance, or Chinook. It can imitate anything—that is, become anything. If it had reached the Antarctic Sea, it would have become a seal, maybe two seals. They might have attacked a killer whale, and become either killers, or a herd of seals. Or maybe it would have caught an albatross, or a skua gull, and flown to South America."

Norris cursed softly. "And every time, it digested something, and imitated it—"

"It would have had its original bulk left, to start again," Blair finished. "Nothing would kill it. It has no natural enemies, because it becomes whatever it wants to. If a killer whale attacked, it would become a killer whale. If it was an albatross, and an eagle attacked it, it would become an eagle. Lord, it might become a female eagle. Go back—build a nest and lay eggs!"

"Are you sure that thing from hell is dead?" Dr. Copper asked softly.

"Yes, thank Heaven," the little biologist gasped. "After they drove the dogs off, I stood there poking Bar's electrocution thing into it for five minutes. It's dead and—cooked."

"Then we can only give thanks that this is Antarctica, where there is not one, single, solitary, living thing for it to imitate, except these animals in camp."

"Us," Blair giggled. "It can imitate us. Dogs can't make four hundred miles to the sea; there's no food. There aren't any skua gulls to imitate at this season. There aren't any Penguins this far inland. There's nothing that can reach the sea from this point—except us. We've got the brains. We can do it. Don't you see—*it's got to imitate us—it's got to be one of us—that's the only way it can fly an airplane—fly a plane for two hours, and rule—be—all Earth's inhabitants.* A world for the taking—*if it imitates us!*

"It didn't know yet. It hadn't had a chance to learn. It was rushed—hurried—took the thing nearest its own size. Look—I'm Pandora! I opened the box! And the only hope that can come out is—that nothing can come out. You didn't see me. I did It. I fixed it. I smashed every magneto. Not a plane can fly. Nothing can fly." Blair giggled and lay down on the floor crying.

Chief Pilot Van Wall made a dive for the door. His feet were fading echoes in the corridors as Dr. Copper bent unhurriedly over the little man on the floor. From his office at the end of the room he brought something, and injected a solution into Blair's arm. "He might come out of it when he wakes up," he sighed rising. McReady helped him lift the biologist onto a near-by bunk. "It all depends on whether we can convince him that thing is dead."

Van Wall ducked into the shack brushing his heavy blond beard absently. "I didn't think a biologist would do a thing like that up thoroughly. He missed the spares in the second cache. It's all right. I smashed them."

Commander Garry nodded. "I was wondering about the radio."

Dr. Copper snorted. "You don't think it can leak

out on a radio wave, do you? You'd have five rescue attempts in the next three months if you stop the broadcasts. The thing to do is talk loud and not make a sound. Now I wonder—"

McReady looked speculatively at the doctor. "It might be like an infectious disease. Everything that drank, any of its blood—"

Copper shook his head. "Blair missed something. Imitate it may, but it has, to a certain extent, its own body-chemistry, its own metabolism. If it didn't it would become a dog—and be a dog and nothing more. It has to be an imitation dog. Therefore you can detect it by serum tests. And its chemistry, since it comes from another world, must be so wholly, radically different that a few cells, such as gained by drops of blood, would be treated as disease germs by the dog, or human body."

"Blood—would one of those imitations bleed?" Norris demanded.

"Surely. Nothing mystic about blood. Muscle is about 90 percent water; blood differs only in having a couple percent more water, and less connective tissue. They'd bleed all right," Copper assured him.

Blair sat up in his bunk suddenly. "Connant—where's Connant?"

The physicist moved over toward the little biologist. "Here I am. What do you want?"

"Are You?" giggled Blair. He lapsed back into the bunk contorted with silent laughter.

Connant looked at him blankly. "Huh? Am I what?"

"*Are* you there?" Blair burst into gales of laughter. "*Are* you Connant? The beast wanted to be a *man*— not a dog—"

SEVEN

DR. COPPER ROSE WEARILY from the bunk, and washed the hypodermic carefully. The little tinkles it made seemed loud in the packed room, now that Blair's gurgling laughter had finally quieted. Copper looked toward Garry and shook his head slowly. "Hopeless, I'm afraid. I don't think we can ever convince him the thing is dead now."

Norris laughed uncertainly. "I'm not sure you can convince me. Oh, damn you, McReady."

"McReady?" Commander Garry turned to look from Norris to McReady curiously.

"The nightmares," Norris explained. "He had a theory about the nightmares we had at the Secondary Station after finding that thing."

"And that was?" Garry looked at McReady levelly.

Norris answered for him, jerkily, uneasily. "That the creature wasn't dead, had a sort of enormously slowed existence, an existence that permitted it, nonetheless, to be vaguely aware of the passing of time, of our coming, after endless years. I had a dream it could imitate things."

"Well," Copper grunted, "it can."

"Don't be an ass," Norris snapped. "That's not what's bothering me. In the dream it could read minds, read thoughts and ideas and mannerisms."

"What's so bad about that? It seems to be worrying you more than the thought of the joy we're going to have with a mad man in an Antarctic camp." Copper nodded toward Blair's sleeping form.

McReady shook his great head slowly. "You know that Connant is Connant, because he not merely looks like Connant—which we're beginning to believe that beast might be able to do—but he thinks like Connant, talks like Connant, moves himself around as Connant does. That takes more than merely a body that looks like him; that takes Connant's own mind, and thoughts and mannerisms. Therefore, though you know that the thing might make itself *look* like Connant, you aren't much bothered, because you know it has a mind from another world, a totally unhuman mind, that couldn't possibly react and think and talk like a man we know, and do it so well as to fool us for a moment. The idea of the creature imitating one of us is fascinating, but unreal because it is too completely unhuman to deceive us. It doesn't have a human mind."

"As I said before," Norris repeated, looking steadily at McReady, "you can say the damnedest things at the damnedest times. Will you be so good as to finish that thought—one way or the other?"

Kinner, the scar-faced expedition cook, had been standing near Connant. Suddenly he moved down the length of the crowded room toward his familiar galley. He shook the ashes from the galley stove noisily.

"It would do it no good," said Dr. Copper, softly as though thinking out loud, "to merely look like something it was trying to imitate; it would have to understand its feelings, its reaction. It *is* unhuman; it has powers of imitation beyond any conception of man. A good actor, by training himself, can imitate another man, another man's mannerisms, well enough to fool most people. Of course no actor could imitate so perfectly as to deceive men who had been living with the imitated one in the complete lack of privacy of an Antarctic camp. That would take a super-human skill."

"Oh, you've got the bug too?" Norris cursed softly.

Connant, standing alone at one end of the room, looked about him wildly, his face white. A gentle eddying of the men had crowded them slowly down toward the other end of the room, so that he stood quite alone. "My God, will you two Jeremiahs shut up?" Connant's voice shook. "What am I? Some kind of a microscopic specimen you're dissecting?

Some unpleasant worm you're discussing in the third person?"

McReady looked up at him; his slowly twisting hand stopped for a moment. "Having a lovely time. Wish you were here. Signed: Everybody.

"Connant, if you think you're having a hell of a time, just move over on the other end for a while. You've got one thing we haven't; you know what the answer is. I'll tell you this, right now you're the most feared and respected man in Big Magnet."

"Lord, I wish you could see your eyes," Connant gasped. "Stop staring, will you! What the hell are you going to do?"

"Have you any suggestions, Dr. Copper?" Commander Garry asked steadily. "The present situation is impossible."

"Oh, is it?" Connant snapped. "Come over here and look at that crowd. By Heaven, they look exactly like that gang of huskies around the corridor bend. Benning, will you stop hefting that damned ice-ax?"

The coppery blade rang on the floor as the aviation mechanic nervously dropped it. He bent over and picked it up instantly, hefting it slowly, turning it in his hands, his browns eyes moving jerkily about the room.

Copper sat down on the bunk beside Blair. The wood creaked noisily in the room. Far down a corridor, a dog yelped in pain, and the dogdrivers' tense voices floated softly back. "Microscopic examination," said the doctor thoughtfully, "would be useless, as Blair pointed out. Considerable time has passed. However, serum tests would be definitive."

"Serum tests? What do you mean exactly?" Commander Garry asked.

"If I had a rabbit that had been injected with human blood—a poison to rabbits, of course, as is the blood of any animal save that of another rabbit—and the injections continued in increasing doses for some time, the rabbit would be human-immune. If a small quantity of its blood were drawn off, allowed to separate in a test-tube, and to the clear serum, a bit of human blood were added, there would be a visible reaction, proving the blood was human. If cow, or dog blood were added—or any protein material other than that one thing, human blood—no reaction would take place. That would prove definitely."

"Can you suggest where I might catch a rabbit for you, Doc?" Norris asked. "That is, nearer than Australia; we don't want to waste time going that far."

"I know there aren't any rabbits in Antarctica," Copper nodded, "but that is simply the usual animal. Any animal except man will do. A dog for instance. But it will take several days, and due to the greater size of the animal, considerable blood. Two of us will have to contribute."

"Would I do?" Garry asked.

"That will make two," Copper nodded. "I'll get to work on it right away."

"What about Connant in the meantime?" Kinner

demanded. "I'm going out that door and head off for the Ross Sea before I cook for him."

"He may be human—" Copper started.

Connant burst out in a flood of curses. "Human! *May* be human, you damned saw bones! What in hell do you think I am?"

"A monster," Copper snapped sharply. "Now shut up and listen." Connant's face drained of color and he sat down heavily as the indictment was put in words. "Until we know—you know as well as we do that we have reason to question the fact, and only you know how that question is to be answered—we may reasonably be expected to lock you up. If you are—unhuman—you're a lot more dangerous than poor Blair there, and I'm going to see that he's locked up thoroughly. I expect that his next stage will be a violent desire to kill you, all the dogs, and probably all of us. When he wakes, he will be convinced we're all unhuman, and nothing on the planet will ever change his conviction. It would be kinder to let him die, but we can't do that, of course. He's going in one shack, and you can stay in Cosmos House with your cosmic ray apparatus. Which is about what you'd do anyway. I've got to fix up a couple of dogs."

Connant nodded bitterly. "I'm human. Hurry that test. Your eyes—Lord, I wish you could see your eyes staring—"

Commander Garry watched anxiously as Clark, the doghandler, held the big brown Alaskan husky, while Copper began the injection treatment. The dog was not anxious to cooperate; the needle was painful, and already he'd experienced considerable needle work that morning. Five stitches held closed a slash that ran from his shoulder across the ribs half way down his body. One long fang was broken off short; the missing part was to be found half-buried in the shoulder bone of the monstrous thing on the table in the Ad Building.

"How long will that take?" Garry asked, pressing his arm gently. It was sore from the prick of the needle Dr. Copper had used to withdraw blood.

Copper shrugged. "I don't know, to be frank. I know the general method, I've used it on rabbits. But I haven't experimented with dogs. They're big, clumsy animals to work with; naturally rabbits are preferable, and serve ordinarily. In civilized places you can buy a stock of human-immune rabbits from suppliers, and not many investigators take the trouble to prepare their own."

"What do they want with them back there?" Clark asked.

"Criminology is one large field. A says he didn't murder B, but that the blood on his shirt came from killing a chicken. The State makes a test, then it's up to A to explain how it is the blood reacts on human-immune rabbits, but not on chicken-immunes."

"What are we going to do with Blair in the meantime?" Garry asked wearily. "It's all right to let him sleep where he is for a while, but when he wakes up—"

"Barclay and Benning are fitting some bolts on the door of Cosmos House," Copper replied grimly.

"Connant's acting like a gentleman. I think perhaps the way the other men look at him makes him rather want privacy. Lord knows, heretofore we've all of us individually prayed for a little privacy."

Clark laughed bitterly. "Not any more, thank you. The more the merrier."

"Blair," Copper went on, "will also have to have privacy—and locks. He's going to have a pretty definite plan in mind when he wakes up. Ever hear the old story of how to stop hoof-and-mouth disease in cattle?"

"If there isn't any hoof-and-mouth disease, there won't be any hoof-and-mouth disease," Copper explained. "You get rid of it by killing every animal that exhibits it, and every animal that's been near the diseased animal. Blair's a biologist, and knows that story. He's afraid of this thing we loosed. The answer is probably pretty clear in his mind now. Kill everybody and everything in this camp before a skua gull or a wandering albatross coming in with the spring chances out this way and—catches the disease."

Clark's lips curled in a twisted grin. "Sounds logical to me. If things get too bad—maybe we'd better let Blair get loose. It would save us committing suicide. We might also make something of a vow that if things get bad, we see that that does happen."

Copper laughed softly. "The last man alive in Big Magnet—wouldn't be a man," he pointed out. "Somebody's got to kill those—creatures that don't desire to kill themselves, you know. We don't have enough thermite to do it all at once, and the decanite explosive wouldn't help much. I have an idea that even small pieces of one of those beings would be self-sufficient."

"If," said Garry thoughtfully, "they can modify their protoplasm at will, won't they simply modify themselves to birds and fly away? They can read all about birds, and imitate their structure without even meeting them. Or imitate, perhaps, birds of their home planet."

Copper shook his head, and helped Clark to free the dog. "Man studied birds for centuries, trying to learn how to make a machine to fly like them. He never did do the trick; his final success came when he broke away entirely and tried new methods. Knowing the general idea, and knowing the detailed structure of wing and bone and nerve-tissue is something far, far different. And as for other-world birds, perhaps, in fact very probably, the atmospheric conditions here are so vastly different that their birds couldn't fly. Perhaps, even, the being came from a planet like Mars with such a thin atmosphere that there were no birds."

Barclay came into the building, trailing a length of airplane control cable. "It's finished, Doc. Cosmo House can't be opened from the inside. Now where do we put Blair?"

Copper looked toward Garry. "There wasn't any biology building. I don't know where we can isolate him."

"How about East Cache?" Garry said after a moment's thought. "Will Blair be able to look after himself—or need attention?"

"He'll be capable enough. We'll be the ones to watch out," Copper assured him grimly. "Take a stove, a couple of bags of coal, necessary supplies and a few tools to fix it up. Nobody's been out there since last fall, have they?"

Garry shook his head. "If he gets noisy—I thought that might be a good idea."

Barclay hefted the tools he was carrying and looked up at Garry. "If the muttering he's doing now is any sign, he's going to sing away the night hours. And we won't like his song."

"What's he saying?" Copper asked.

Barclay shook his head. "I didn't care to listen much. You can if you want to. But I gathered that the blasted idiot had all the dreams McReady had, and a few more. He slept beside the thing when we stopped on the trail coming in from Secondary Magnetic, remember. He dreamt the thing was alive, and dreamt more details. And—damn his soul— knew it wasn't all dream, or had reason to. He knew it had telepathic powers that were stirring vaguely, and that it could not only read minds, but project thoughts. They weren't dreams, you see. They were stray thoughts that thing was broadcasting, the way Blair's broadcasting his thoughts now—a sort of telepathic muttering in its sleep. That's why he knew so much about its powers. I guess you and I, Doc, weren't so sensitive—if you want to believe in telepathy."

"I have to," Copper sighed. "Dr. Rhine of Duke University has shown that it exists, shown that some are much more sensitive than others."

"Well, if you want to learn a lot of details, go listen in on Blair's broadcast. He's driven most of the boys out of the Ad Building; Kinner's rattling pans like coal going down a chute. When he can't rattle a pan, he shakes ashes.

"By the way, Commander, what are we going to do this spring, now the planes are out of it?"

Garry sighed. "I'm afraid our expedition is going to be a loss. We cannot divide our strength now."

"It won't be a loss—if we continue to live, and come out of this," Copper promised him. "The find we've made, if we can get it under control, is important enough. The cosmic ray data, magnetic work, and atmospheric work won't be greatly hindered."

Garry laughed mirthlessly. "I was just thinking of the radio broadcasts. Telling half the world about the wonderful results of our exploration flights, trying to fool men like Byrd and Ellsworth back home there that we're doing something."

Copper nodded gravely. "They'll know something's wrong. But men like that have judgment enough to know we wouldn't do tricks without some sort of reason, and will wait for our return to judge us. I think it comes to this: men who know enough to recognize our deception will wait for our return. Men who haven't discretion and faith enough to wait will not have the experience to detect any fraud. We know enough of the conditions here to put through a good bluff."

"Just so they don't send 'rescue' expeditions," Garry

prayed. "When—if—we're ever ready to come out, we'll have to send word to Captain Forsythe to bring a stock of magnetos with him when he comes down. But—never mind that."

"You mean if we don't come out?" asked Barclay. "I was wondering if a nice running account of an eruption or an earthquake via radio—with a swell windup by using a stick of decanite under the microphone—would help. Nothing, of course, will entirely keep people out. One of those swell, melodramatic 'last-man-alive-scenes' might make 'em go easy though."

Garry smiled with genuine humor. "Is everybody in camp trying to figure that out too?"

Copper laughed. "What do you think, Garry? We're confident we can win out. But not too easy about it, I guess."

Clark grinned up from the dog he was petting into calmness. "Confident, did you say, Doc?"

EIGHT

BLAIR MOVED RESTLESSLY around the small shack. His eyes jerked and quivered in vague, fleeting glances at the four men with him; Barclay, six feet tall and weighing over 190 pounds; McReady, a bronze giant of a man; Dr. Copper, short, squatly powerful; and Benning, five-feet-ten of wiry strength.

Blair was huddled up against the far wall of the East Cache cabin, his gear piled in the middle of the floor beside the heating stove, forming an island between him and the four men. His bony hands clenched and fluttered, terrified. His pale eyes wavered uneasily as his bald, freckled head darted about in birdlike motion.

"I don't want anybody coming here. I'll cook my

own food," he snapped nervously. "Kinner may be human now, but I don't believe it. I'm going to get out of here, but I'm not going to eat any food you send me. I want cans. Sealed cans."

"O.K., Blair, we'll bring 'em tonight," Barclay promised. "You've got coal, and the fire's started. I'll make a last—" Barclay started forward.

Blair instantly scurried to the farthest corner. "Get out! Keep away from me, you monster!" the little biologist shrieked, and tried to claw his way through the wall of the shack. "Keep away from me—keep away—I won't be absorbed—I won't be—"

Barclay relaxed and moved back. Dr. Copper shook his head. "Leave him alone, Bar. It's easier for him to fix the thing himself. We'll have to fix the door, I think—"

The four men let themselves out. Efficiently, Benning and Barclay fell to work. There were no locks in Antarctica; there wasn't enough privacy to make them needed. But powerful screws had been driven in each side of the door frame, and the spare aviation control cable, immensely strong, woven steel wire, was rapidly caught between them and drawn taut. Barclay went to work with a drill and a keyhole saw. Presently he had a trap cut in the door through which goods could be passed without unlashing the entrance. Three powerful hinges from a stock-crate, two hasps and a pair of three-inch cotter-pins made it proof against opening from the other side.

Blair moved about restlessly inside. He was

dragging something over to the door with panting gasps and muttering, frantic curses. Barclay opened the hatch and glanced in, Dr. Copper peering over his shoulder. Blair had moved the heavy bunk against the door. It could not be opened without his cooperation now.

"Don't know but what the poor man's right at that," McReady sighed. "If he gets loose, it is his avowed intention to kill each and all of us as quickly as possible, which is something we don't agree with. But we've something on our side of that door that is worse than a homicidal maniac. If one or the other has to get loose, I think I'll come up and undo those lashings here."

Barclay grinned. "You let me know, and I'll show you how to get these off fast. Let's go back."

The sun was painting the northern horizon in multi-colored rainbows still, though it was two hours below the horizon. The field of drift swept off to the north, sparkling under its flaming colors in a million reflected glories. Low mounds of rounded white on the northern horizon showed the Magnet Range was barely awash above the sweeping drift. Little eddies of wind-lifted snow swirled away from their skis as they set out toward the main encampment two miles away. The spidery finger of the broadcast radiator lifted a gaunt black needle against the white of the Antarctic continent. The snow under their skies was like fine sand, hard and gritty.

"Spring," said Benning bitterly, "is come. Ain't we

got fun! And I've been looking forward to getting away from this blasted hole in the ice."

"I wouldn't try it now, if I were you." Barclay grunted. "Guys that set out from here in the next few days are going to be marvelously unpopular."

"How is your dog getting along, Dr. Copper?" McReady asked. "Any results yet?"

"In thirty hours? I wish there were. I gave him an injection of my blood today. But I imagine another five days will be needed. I don't know certainly enough to stop sooner."

"I've been wondering—if Connant were—changed, would he have warned us so soon after the animal escaped? Wouldn't he have waited long enough for it to have a real chance to fix itself? Until we woke up naturally?" McReady asked slowly.

"The thing is selfish. You didn't think it looked as though it were possessed of a store of the higher justices, did you?" Dr. Copper pointed out. "Every part of it is all of it, every part of it is all for itself, I imagine. If Connant were changed, to save his skin, he'd have to—but Connant's feelings aren't changed; they're imitated perfectly, or they're his own. Naturally, the imitation, imitating perfectly Connant's feelings, would do exactly what Connant would do."

"Say, couldn't Norris or Van give Connant some kind of a test? If the thing is brighter than men, it might know more physics than Connant should, and they'd catch it out," Barclay suggested.

Copper shook his head wearily. "Not if it reads

minds. You can't plan a trap for it. Van suggested that last night. He hoped it would answer some of the questions of physics he'd like to know answers to."

"This expedition-of-four idea is going to make life happy." Benning looked at his companions. "Each of us with an eye on the others to make sure he doesn't do something—peculiar. Man, aren't we going to be a trusting bunch! Each man eyeing his neighbors with the grandest exhibition of faith and trust—I'm beginning to know what Connant meant by 'I wish you could see your eyes.' Every now and then we all have it, I guess. One of you looks around with a sort of 'I-wonder-if-the-other-*three*-are-look.' Incidentally, I'm not excepting myself."

"So far as we know, the animal is dead, with a slight question as to Connant. No other is suspected," McReady stated slowly. "The 'always-four' order is merely a precautionary measure."

"I'm waiting for Garry to make it four-in-a-bunk," Barclay sighed. "I thought I didn't have any privacy before, but since that order—"

NINE

NONE WATCHED MORE TENSELY

than Connant. A little sterile glass test-tube, half-filled with straw-colored fluid. One-two-three-four-five drops of the clear solution Dr. Copper had prepared from the drops of blood from Connant's arm. The tube was shaken carefully, then set in a beaker of clear, warm water. The thermometer read blood heat, a little thermostat clicked noisily, and the electric hotplate began to glow as the lights flickered slightly. Then—little white flecks of precipitation were forming, snowing down in the clear straw-colored fluid. "Lord," said Connant. He dropped heavily into a bunk, crying like a baby. "Six days—" Connant sobbed, "six days in there—wondering if that damned test would lie—"

Garry moved over silently, and slipped his arm across the physicist's back.

"It couldn't lie," Dr. Copper said, "The dog was human-immune—and the serum reacted."

"He's—all right?" Norris gasped. "Then—the animal is dead—dead forever?"

"He is human," Copper spoke definitely, "and the animal is dead."

Kinner burst out laughing, laughing hysterically: McReady turned toward him and slapped his face with a methodical one-two, one-two action. The cook laughed, gulped, cried a moment, and sat up rubbing his checks, mumbling his thanks vaguely. "I was scared. Lord, I was scared—"

Norris laughed bitterly. "You think we weren't, you ape? You think maybe Connant wasn't?"

The Ad Building stirred with a sudden rejuvenation. Voices laughed, the men clustering around Connant spoke with unnecessarily loud voices, jittery, nervous voices relievedly friendly again. Somebody called out a suggestion, and a dozen started for their skis. Blair. Blair might recover—Dr. Copper fussed with his test-tubes in nervous relief, trying solutions. The party of relief for Blair's shack started out the door, skis clapping noisily. Down the corridor, the dogs set up a quick yelping howl as the air of excited relief reached them.

Dr. Copper fussed with his tubes. McReady noticed him first, sitting on the edge of the bunk, with two precipitin-whitened test-tubes of straw-colored fluid, his face whiter than the stuff in the tubes, silent tears slipping down from horror-widened eyes.

McReady felt a cold knife of fear pierce through his heart and freeze in his breast. Dr. Copper looked up. "Garry," he called hoarsely. "Garry, for God's sake, come here."

Commander Garry walked toward him sharply. Silence clapped down on the Ad Building. Connant looked up, rose stiffly from his seat.

"Garry—tissue from the monster—precipitates too. It proves nothing. Nothing but—but the dog was monster-immune too. That one of the two contributing blood—one of us two, you and I, Garry—*one of us is a monster.*"

TEN

"BAR, CALL BACK those men before they tell Blair," McReady said quietly. Blair went to the door; faintly his shouts came back to the tensely silent men in the room. Then he was back.

"They're coming," he said. "I didn't tell them why. Just that Dr. Copper said not to go."

"McReady," Garry sighed, "you're in command now. May God help you. I cannot."

The bronzed giant nodded slowly, his deep eyes on Commander Garry.

"I may be the one," Garry added. "I know I'm not, but I cannot prove it to you in any way. Dr. Copper's test has broken down. The fact that he showed it was useless, when it was to the advantage of the monster to have that uselessness not known, would seem to prove he was human."

Copper rocked back and forth slowly on the bunk. "I know I'm human. I can't prove it either. One of us two is a liar, for that test cannot lie, and it says one of us is. I gave proof that the test was wrong, which seems to prove I'm human, and now Garry has given that argument which proves me human—which he, as the monster, should not do. Round and round and round and round and—"

Dr. Copper's head, then his neck and shoulders began circling slowly in time to the words. Suddenly he was lying back on the bunk, roaring with laughter. "It doesn't have to prove one of us is a monster! It doesn't have to prove that at all! Ho-ho. If we're *all* monsters it works the same! We're all monsters—all of us—Connant and Garry and I—and all of you."

"McReady," Van Wall, the blond-bearded Chief Pilot, called softly. "you were on the way to an M.D. when you took up meteorology, weren't you? Can you make some kind of test?"

McReady went over to Copper slowly, took the hypodermic from his hand, and washed it carefully in ninety-five percent alcohol. Garry sat on the bunk edge with wooden face, watching Copper and McReady expressionlessly. "What Copper said is possible," McReady sighed. "Van, will you help here? Thanks." The filled needle jabbed into Copper's thigh. The man's laughter did not stop, but slowly faded into sobs, then sound sleep as the morphia took hold.

McReady turned again. The men who had started

for Blair stood at the far end of the room, skis dripping snow, their faces as white as their skis. Connant had a lighted cigarette in each hand; one he was puffing absently, and staring at the floor. The heat of the one in his left hand attracted him and he stared at it, and the one in the other hand stupidly for a moment. He dropped one and crushed it under his heel slowly.

"Dr. Copper," McReady repeated, "could be right. I know I'm human—but of course can't prove it. I'll repeat the test for my own information. Any of you others who wish to may do the same."

Two minutes later, McReady held a test-tube with white precipitin settling slowly from straw-colored serum. "It reacts to human blood too, so they aren't both monsters."

"I didn't think they were," Van Wall sighed. "That wouldn't suit the monster either; we could have destroyed them if we knew. Why hasn't the monster destroyed us, do you suppose? It seems to be loose."

McReady snorted. Then laughed softly. "Elementary, my dear Watson. The monster wants to have life-forms available. It cannot animate a dead body, apparently. It is just waiting—waiting until the best opportunities come. We who remain human, it is holding in reserve."

Kinner shuddered violently. "Hey. Hey, Mac. Mac, would I know if I was a monster? Would I know if the monster had already got me? Oh Lord, I may be a monster already."

"You'd know, " McReady answered.

"But we wouldn't," Norris laughed shortly, half-hysterically.

McReady looked at the vial of serum remaining. "There's one thing this damned stuff is good for, at that," he said thoughtfully. "Clark, will you and Van help me? The rest of the gang better stick together here. Keep an eye on each other," he said bitterly. "See that you don't get into mischief, shall we say?"

McReady started down the tunnel toward Dog Town, with Clark and Van Wall behind him. "You need more serum?" Clark asked.

McReady shook his head. "Tests. There's four cows and a bull, and nearly seventy dogs down there. This stuff reacts only to human blood and—monsters."

ELEVEN

MCREADY CAME BACK to the Ad Building and went silently to the wash stand. Clark and Van Wall joined him a moment later. Clark's lips had developed a tic, jerking into sudden, unexpected sneers.

"What did you do?" Connant exploded suddenly. "More immunizing?"

Clark snickered, and stopped with a hiccough. "Immunizing. Haw! Immune all right."

"That monster," said Van Wall steadily, "is quite logical. Our immune dog was quite all right, and we drew a little more serum for the tests. But we won't make any more."

"Can't—can't you use one man's blood or another dog—" Norris began.

"There aren't," said McReady softly, "any more dogs. Nor cattle, I might add."

"No more dogs?" Benning sat down slowly.

"They're very nasty when they start changing," Van Wall said precisely, "but slow. That electrocution iron you made up, Barclay, is very fast. There is only one dog left—our immune. The monster left that for us, so we could play with our little test. The rest—" He shrugged and dried his hands.

"The cattle—" gulped Kinner.

"Also. Reacted very nicely. They look funny as hell when they start melting. The beast hasn't any quick escape, when it's tied in dog chains, or halters, and it had to be to imitate."

Kinner stood up slowly. His eyes darted around the room, and came to rest horribly quivering on a tin bucket in the galley. Slowly, step by step. he retreated toward the door, his mouth opening and closing silently, like a fish out of water.

"The milk—" he gasped. "I milked 'em an hour ago—" His voice broke into a scream as he dived through the door. He was out on the ice cap without windproof or heavy clothing.

Van Wall looked after him for a moment thoughtfully. "He's probably hopelessly mad," he said at length, "but he might be a monster escaping. He hasn't skis. Take a blowtorch—in case."

The physical motion of the chase helped them; something that needed doing. Three of the other men were quietly being sick. Norris was lying flat on his back, his face greenish, looking steadily at the bottom of the bunk above him.

"Mac, how long have the—cows been not-cows."

McReady shrugged his shoulders hopelessly. He went over to the milk bucket, and with his little tube of serum went to work on it. The milk clouded it, making certainty difficult. Finally he dropped the test-tube in the stand and shook his head. "It tests negatively. Which means either they were cows then, or that, being perfect imitations, they gave perfectly good milk."

Copper stirred restlessly in his sleep and gave a gurgling cross between a snore and a laugh. Silent eyes fastened on him. "Would morphia—a monster—" somebody started to ask.

"Lord knows," McReady shrugged. "It affects every Earthly animal I know of."

Connant suddenly raised his head. "Mac! The dogs must have swallowed pieces of the monster, and the pieces destroyed them! The dogs were where the monster resided. I was locked up. Doesn't that prove—"

Van Wall shook his head. "Sorry. Proves nothing about what you are, only proves what you didn't do."

"It doesn't do that," McReady sighed. "We are helpless. Because we don't know enough, and so jittery we don't think straight. Locked up! Ever watch a white corpuscle of the blood go through the wall of a blood vessel? No? It sticks out a pseudopod.

And there it is—on the far side of the wall."

"Oh," said Van Wall unhappily. "The cattle tried to melt down, didn't they? The could have melted down—become just a thread of stuff and leaked under a door to re-collect on the other side. Ropes—no—no, that wouldn't do it. They couldn't live in a sealed tank or—"

"If," said McReady, "you shoot it through the heart, and it doesn't die, it's a monster. That's the best test I can think of, offhand."

"No dogs," said Garry quietly, "and no cattle. It has to imitate men now. And locking up doesn't do any good. Your test might work, Mac, but I am afraid it would be hard on the men."

TWELVE

CLARK LOOKED UP from the galley stove as Van Wall, Barclay, McReady and Benning came in, brushing the drift from their clothes. The other men jammed into the Ad Building continued studiously to do as they were doing, playing chess, poker, reading. Ralsen was fixing a sledge on the table; Van and Norris had their heads together over magnetic data, while Harvey read tables in a low voice.

Dr. Copper snored softly on the bunk. Garry was working with Dutton over a sheaf of radio messages on the corner of Dutton's bunk and a small fraction of the radio table. Connant was using most of the table for Cosmic Ray sheets.

Quite plainly through the corridor, despite two closed doors, they could hear Kinner's voice. Clark banged a kettle onto the galley stove and beckoned McReady silently. The meterologist went over to him.

"I don't mind the cooking so damn much," Clark said nervously, "but isn't there some way to stop that bird? We all agreed that it would be safe to move him into Cosmos House."

"Kinner?" McReady nodded toward the door. "I'm afraid not. I can dope him, I suppose, but we don't have an unlimited supply of morphia, and he's not in danger of losing his mind. Just hysterical."

"Well, we're in danger of losing ours. You've been out for an hour and a half. That's been going on steadily ever since, and it was going for two hours before. There's a limit, you know."

Garry wandered over slowly, apologetically. For an instant, McReady caught the feral spark of fear—horror—in Clark's eyes, and knew at the same instant it was in his own. Garry—Garry or Copper—was certainly a monster.

"If you could stop that, I think it would be a sound policy, Mac," Garry spoke quietly. "There are—tensions enough in this room. We agreed that it would be safe for Kinner in there, because everyone else in camp is under constant eyeing." Garry shivered slightly. "And try, try in God's name, to find some test that will work."

McReady sighed. "Watched or unwatched, everyone's tense. Blair's jammed the trap so it won't open now. Says he's got food enough, and keeps screaming 'Go away, go away—you're monsters. I won't be absorbed. I won't. I'll tell men when they come. Go away.' So—we went away."

"There's no other test?" Garry pleaded.

McReady shrugged his shoulders. "Copper was perfectly right. The serum test could be absolutely definitive if it hadn't been—contaminated. But that's the only dog left, and he's fixed now."

"Chemicals? Chemical tests?"

McReady shook his head. "Our chemistry isn't that good. I tried the microscope, you know."

Garry nodded. "Monster-dog and real dog were identical. But—you've got to go on. What are we going to do after dinner?"

Van Wall joined them quietly. "Rotation sleeping. Half the crowd asleep; half awake. I wonder how many of us are monsters? All the dogs were. We thought we were safe, but somehow it got Copper—or you." Van Wall's eyes flashed uneasily. "It may have gotten every one of you—all of you but myself may be wondering, looking. No, that's not possible. You'd just spring then. I'd be helpless. We humans might somehow have the greater number now. But—" he stopped.

McReady laughed shortly. "You're doing what Norris complained of in me. Leaving it hanging. 'But if one more is changed—that may shift the balance of power.' It doesn't fight. I don't think it ever fights. It must be a peaceable thing, in its own—inimitable way. It never had to, because it always gained its end—otherwise."

Van Wall's mouth twisted in a sickly grin. "You're

suggesting then, that perhaps it already has the greater numbers, but is just waiting—waiting, all of them—all of you, for all I know—waiting till I, the last human, drop my wariness in sleep. Mac, did you notice their eyes, all looking at us?"

Garry sighed. "You haven't been sitting here for four straight hours, while all their eyes silently weighed the information that one of us two, Copper or I, is a monster certainly—perhaps both of us."

Clark repeated his request. "Will you stop that bird's noise? He's driving me nuts. Make him tone down, anyway."

"Still praying?" McReady asked.

"Still praying," Clark groaned. "He hasn't stopped for a second. I don't mind his praying if it relieves him, but he yells, he sings psalms and hymns and shouts prayers. He thinks God can't hear well way down here."

"Maybe He can't," Barclay grunted. "Or He'd have done something about this thing loosed from hell."

"Somebody's going to try that test you mentioned, if you don't stop him," Clark stated grimly. "I think a cleaver in the head would be as positive a test as a bullet in the heart."

"Go ahead with the food. I'll see what I can do. There may be something in the cabinets." McReady moved wearily toward the corner Copper had used as his dispensary. Three tall cabinets of rough boards, two locked, were the repositories of the camp's medical supplies. Twelve years ago, McReady had graduated, had started for an internship, and been diverted to meteorology. Copper was a picked man, a man who knew his profession thoroughly and modernly. More than half the drugs available were totally unfamiliar to McReady; many of the others he had forgotten. There was no huge medical library here, no series of journals available to learn the things he had forgotten, the elementary, simple things to Copper, things that did not merit inclusion in the small library he had been forced to content himself with. Books are heavy, and every ounce of supplies had been freighted in by air.

McReady picked a barbituate hopefully. Barclay and Van went with him. One man never went anywhere alone in Big Magnet.

Ralsen had his sledge put away, and the physicists had moved off the table, the poker game broken up when they got back. Clark was putting out the food. The click of spoons and the muffled sounds of eating were the only sign of life in the room. There were no words spoken as the three returned; simply all eyes focused on them questioningly, while the jaw moved methodically.

McReady stiffened suddenly. Kinner was screeching out a hymn in a hoarse, cracked voice. He looked wearily at Van Wall with a twisted grin and shook his head. "Hu-uh."

Van Wall cursed bitterly, and sat down at the table. "We'll just plumb have to take that till his voice wears out. He can't yell like that forever."

"He's got a brass throat and a cast-iron larynx," Norris declared savagely. "Then we could be hopeful, and suggest he's one of our friends. In that case he could go on renewing his throat till doomsday."

Silence clamped down. For twenty minutes they ate without a word. Then Connant jumped up with an angry violence. "You sit as still as a bunch of graven images. You don't say a word, but oh Lord, what expressive eyes you've got. They roll around like a bunch of glass marbles spilling down a table. They wink and blink and stare—and whisper things. Can you guys look somewhere else for a change, please?

"Listen, Mac, you're in charge here. Let's run movies for the rest of the night. We've been saving those reels to make 'em last. Last for what? Who is it's going to see those last reels, eh? Let's see 'em while we can, and look at something other than each other.

"Sound idea, Connant. I, for one, am quite willing to change this in any way I can."

"Turn the sound up loud, Dutton. Maybe you can drown out the hymns," Clark suggested.

"But don't," Norris said softly, "don't turn off the lights altogether."

"The lights will be out." McReady shook his head. "We'll show all the cartoon movies we have. You won't mind seeing the old cartoons, will you?"

"Goody, goody—a moom-pitcher show. I'm just in the mood." McReady turned to look at the speaker, a lean, lanky New Englander, by the name of Caldwell. Caldwell was stuffing his pipe slowly, a sour eye cocked up to McReady.

The bronze giant was forced to laugh. "O.K., Bart,

you win. Maybe we aren't quite in the mood for Popeye and trick ducks, but it's something."

"Let's play Classifications," Caldwell suggested slowly. "Or maybe you call it Guggenheim. You draw lines on a piece of paper, and put down classes of things—like animals, you know. One for 'H' and one for 'U' and so on. Like 'Human' and 'Unknown' for instance. I think that would be a hell of a lot better game. Classification, I sort of figure is what we need right now a lot more than movies. Maybe somebody's got a pencil that he can draw lines with, draw lines between the 'U' animals and the 'H' animals for instance."

"McReady's trying to find that kind of pencil," Van Wall answered quietly, "but we've got three kinds of animals here, you know. One that begins with 'M'. We don't want any more."

"Mad ones, you mean. Uh-huh. Clark, I'll help you with those pots so we can get our little peepshow going." Caldwell got up slowly.

Dutton and Barclay and Benning, in charge of the projector and sound mechanism arrangements, went about their job silently, while the Ad Building was cleared and the dishes and pans disposed of. McReady drifted over toward Van Wall slowly, and leaned back in the bunk beside him. "I've been wondering, Van," he said with a wry grin, "whether or not to report my ideas in advance. I forgot the 'U animal' as Caldwell named it, could read minds. I've a vague idea of something that might work. it's too vague to bother with though. Go ahead with your show, while I try to figure out the logic of the thing. I'll take this bunk."

Van Wall glanced up, and nodded. The movie screen would be practically on a line with his bunk, hence making the pictures least distracting here, because least intelligible. "Perhaps you should tell us what you have in mind. As it is, only the unknowns know what you plan. You might be—unknown before you got it into operation."

"Won't take long, if I get it figured out right. But I don't want any more all-but-the-test-dog-monsters things. We better move Copper into this bunk directly above me. He won't be watching the screen either." McReady nodded toward Copper's gently snoring bulk. Garry helped them lift and move the doctor.

McReady leaned back against the bunk, and sank into a trance, almost, of concentration, trying to calculate chances, operations, methods. He was scarcely aware as the others distributed themselves silently, and the screen lit up. Vaguely Kinner's hectic, shouted prayers and his rasping hymn-singing annoyed him till the sound accompaniment started. The lights were turned out, but the large, light-colored areas of the screen reflected enough light for ready visibility. It made men's eyes sparkle as they moved restlessly. Kinner was still praying, shouting, his voice a raucous accompaniment to the mechanical sound. Dutton stepped up the amplification.

So long had the voice been going on, that only

vaguely at first was McReady aware that something seemed missing. Lying as he was, just across the narrow room from the corridor leading to Cosmos House, Kinner's voice had reached him fairly clearly, despite the sound accompaniment of the pictures. It struck him abruptly that it had stopped.

"Dutton, cut that sound," McReady called as he sat up abruptly. The pictures flickered a moment, soundless and strangely futile in the sudden, deep silence. The rising wind on the surface above bubbled melancholy tears of sound down the stove pipes. "Kinner's stopped," McReady said softly.

"For God's sake start that sound then, he may have stopped to listen," Norris snapped.

McReady rose and went down the corridor. Barclay and Van Wall left their places at the far end of the room to follow him. The flickers bulged and twisted on the back of Barclay's gray underwear as he crossed the still-functioning beam of the projector. Dutton snapped on the lights, and the pictures vanished.

Norris stood at the door as McReady had asked. Garry sat down quietly in the bunk nearest the door, forcing Clark to make room for him. Most of the others had stayed exactly where they were. Only Connant walked slowly up and down the room, in steady, unvarying rhythm.

"If you're going to do that, Connant," Clark spat, "we can get along without you altogether, whether you're human or not. Will you stop that damned rhythm?"

"Sorry." The physicist sat down in a bunk, and

watched his toes thoughtfully. It was almost five minutes, five ages while the wind made the only sound, before McReady appeared at the door.

"We," he announced, "haven't got enough grief here already. Somebody's tried to help us out. Kinner has a knife in his throat, which was why he stopped singing, probably. We've got monsters, madmen and murderers. Any more 'M's' you can think of, Caldwell? If there are, we'll probably have 'em before long."

THIRTEEN

"IS BLAIR LOOSE?" someone asked.

"Blair is not loose. Or he flew in. If there's any doubt about where our gentle helper came from—this may clear it up." Van Wall held a footlong, thin-bladed knife in a cloth. The wooden handle was half-burnt, charred with the peculiar pattern of the top of the galley stove.

Clark stared at it. "I did that this afternoon. I forgot the damn thing and left it on the stove."

Van Wall nodded. "I smelled it, if you remember. I knew the knife came from the galley."

"I wonder," said Benning, looking around at the

party warily, "how many more monsters have we? If somebody could slip out of his place, go back of the screen to the galley and then down to the Cosmos House and back—he did come back, didn't he? Yes—everybody's here. Well, if one of the gang could do all that—"

"Maybe a monster did it," Garry suggested quietly. "There's that possibility."

"The monster, as you pointed out today, has only men left to imitate. Would he decrease his—supply, shall we say?" Van Wall pointed out. "No, we just have a plain, ordinary louse, a murderer to deal with. Ordinarily we'd call him an 'inhuman murderer' I suppose, but we have to distinguish now. We have inhuman murderers, and now we have human murderers. Or one at least."

"There's one less human," Norris said softly. "Maybe the monsters have the balance of power now."

"Never mind that," McReady sighed and turned to Barclay. "Bar, will you get your electric gadget? I'm going to make certain—"

Barclay turned down the corridor to get the pronged electrocuter, while McReady and Van Wall went back toward Cosmos House. Barclay followed them in some thirty seconds.

The corridor to Cosmos House twisted, as did nearly all corridors in Big Magnet, and Norris stood at the entrance again. But they heard, rather muffled McReady's sudden shout. There was a savage scurry of blows, dull *ch-thunk, shluff* sounds. "Bar—Bar—" And a curious, savage mewing scream, silenced before even quick-moving Norris had reached the bend.

Kinner—or what had been Kinner—lay on the floor; cut half in two by the great knife McReady had had. The meteorologist stood against the wall, the knife dripping red in his hand. Van Wall was stirring vaguely on the floor, moaning, his hand half-consciously rubbing at his jaw. Barclay, an unutterably savage gleam in his eyes, was methodically leaning on the pronged weapon in his hand, jabbing, jabbing.

Kinner's arms had developed a queer, scaly fur, and the flesh had twisted. The fingers had shortened, the hand rounded, the fingernails become three-inch long things of dull red horn, keened to steel-hard, razor-sharp talons.

McReady raised his head, looked at the knife in his hand and dropped it. "Well, whoever did it can speak up now. He was an inhuman murderer at that—in that he murdered an inhuman. I swear by all that's holy, Kinner was a lifeless corpse on the floor here when we arrived. But when it found we were going to jab it with the power—it changed."

Norris stared unsteadily. "Oh. Lord, those things can act. Ye gods—sitting in here for hours, mouthing prayers to a God it hated! Shouting hymns in a cracked voice—hymns about a Church it never knew. Driving us mad with its ceaseless howling—

"Well. Speak up, whoever did it. You didn't know it, but you did the camp a favor. And I want to know how in blazes you got out of that room without anyone seeing you. It might help in guarding ourselves."

"His screaming—his singing. Even the sound projector couldn't drown it." Clark shivered. "It was a monster."

"Oh," said Van Wall in sudden comprehension. "You were sitting right next to the door, weren't you! And almost behind the projection screen already."

Clark nodded dumbly. "He—it's quiet now. It's a dead—Mac, your test's no damn good. It was dead anyway, monster or man, it was dead."

McReady chuckled softly. "Boys, meet Clark, the only one we know is human! Meet Clark, the one who proves he's human by trying to commit murder—and failing. Will the rest of you please refrain from trying to prove you're human for a while? I think we may have another test."

"A test!" Connant snapped joyfully, then his face sagged in disappointment. "I suppose it's another either-way-you-want-it."

"No," said McReady steadily. "Look sharp and be careful. Come into the Ad Building. Barclay, bring your electrocuter. And somebody—Dutton—stand with Barclay to make sure he does it. Watch every neighbor, for by the Hell these monsters come from, I've got something, and they know it. They're going to get dangerous!"

The group tensed abruptly. An air of crushing menace entered into every man's body, sharply they looked at each other. More keenly than ever before—*is that man next to me an inhuman monster?*

"What is it?" Garry asked, as they stood again in

the main room. "How long will it take?"

"I don't know exactly," said McReady, his voice brittle with angry determination. "But I *know* it will work, and no two ways about it. It depends on a basic quality of the *monsters*, not on us. 'Kinner' just convinced me." He stood heavy and solid in bronzed immobility, completely sure of himself again at last.

"This," said Barclay, hefting the woodenhandled weapon, tipped with its two sharp-pointed, charged conductors, "is going to be rather necessary, I take it. Is the power plant assured?"

Dutton nodded sharply. "The automatic stoker bin is full. The gas power plant is on stand-by. Van Wall and I set it for the movie operation and—we've checked it over rather carefully several times, you know. Anything those wires touch, dies," he assured them grimly "*I* know that."

Dr. Copper stirred vaguely in his bunk, rubbed his eyes with fumbling hand. He sat up slowly, blinked his eyes blurred with sleep and drugs, widened with an unutterable horror of drug-ridden nightmares. "Garry," he mumbled, "Garry—listen. Selfish—from hell they came, and hellish shellfish—I mean self— Do I? What do I mean?" he sank back in his bunk, and snored softly.

McReady looked at him thoughtfully. "We'll know presently," he nodded slowly. "But selfish is what you mean all right. You may have thought of that, half-sleeping, dreaming there. I didn't stop to think what dreams you might be having. But that's all

right. Selfish is the word. They must be, you see."
He turned to the men in the cabin, tense, silent
men staring with wolfish eyes each at his neighbor.
Selfish, and as Dr. Copper said *every part is a whole*.
Every piece is self-sufficient, an animal in itself.

"That, and one other thing, tell the story. There's
nothing mysterious about blood; it's just as normal
a body tissue as a piece of muscle, or a piece of liver.
But it hasn't so much connective tissue, though it
has millions, billions of life-cells."

McReady's great bronze beard ruffled in a grim
smile. "This is satisfying, in a way. I'm pretty
sure we humans still outnumber you—others.
Others standing here. And we have what you,
your otherworld race, evidently doesn't. Not an
imitated, but a bred-in-the-bone instinct, a driving,
unquenchable fire that's genuine. We'll fight, fight
with a ferocity you may attempt to imitate, but
you'll never equal! We're human. We're real. You're
imitations, false to the core of your every cell.

"All right. It's a showdown now. *You* know. You,
with your mind reading. You've lifted the idea from
my brain. You can't do a thing about it.

"Standing here—

"Let it pass. Blood is tissue. They have to bleed, if
they don't bleed when cut, then, by Heaven, they're
phony! Phony from hell! If they bleed—then that
blood, separated from them, is an individual—*a
newly formed individual in its own right, just as they—
split, all of them, from one original, are individuals*!

"Get it, Van? See the answer, Bar?"

Van Wall laughed very softly. "The blood—the blood will not obey. It's a new individual, with all the desire to protect its own life "that the original—the main mass from which it was split—has. The *blood* will live—and try to crawl away from a hot needle, say!"

McReady picked up the scalpel from the table. From the cabinet, he took a rack of test-tubes, a tiny alcohol lamp, and a length of platinum wire set in a little glass rod. A smile of grim satisfaction rode his lips. For a moment he glanced up at those around him. Barclay and Dutton moved toward him slowly, the wooden-handled electric instrument alert.

"Dutton," said McReady, "suppose you stand over by the splice there where you've connected that in. Just make sure nothing pulls it loose."

Dutton moved away. "Now, Van, suppose you be first on this."

White-faced, Van Wall stepped forward. With a delicate precision, McReady cut a vein in the base of his thumb. Van Wall winced slightly, then held steady as a half inch of bright blood collected in the tube. McReady put the tube in the rack, gave Van Wall a bit of alum, and indicated the iodine bottle.

Van Wall stood motionlessly watching. McReady heated the platinum wire in the alcohol lamp flame, then dipped it into the tube. It hissed softly. Five times he repeated the test. "Human, I'd say." McReady sighed, and straightened. "As yet, my theory hasn't been actually proven—but I have hopes. I have hopes.

"Don't, by the way, get too interested in this. We have with us some unwelcome ones, no doubt, Van, will you relieve Barclay at the switch? Thanks. O.K., Barclay, and may I say I hope you stay with us? You're a damned good guy."

Barclay grinned uncertainly; winced under the keen edge of the scalpel. Presently, smiling widely, he retrieved his long-handled weapon.

"Mr. Samuel Dutt—BAR!"

The tensity was released in that second. Whatever of hell the monsters may have had within them, the men in that instant matched it. Barclay had no chance to move his weapon as a score of men poured down on that thing that had seemed Dutton. It mewed, and spat, and tried to grow fangs—and was a hundred broken, torn pieces. Without knives, or any weapon save the brute-given strength of a staff of picked men, the thing was crushed, rent.

Slowly they picked themselves up, their eyes smoldering, very quiet in their emotions. A curious wrinkling of their lips betrayed a species of nervousness.

Barclay went over with the electric weapon. Things smoldered and stank. The caustic acid Van Wall dropped on each spilled drop of blood gave off tickling, cough-provoking fumes.

McReady grinned, his deep-set eyes alight and dancing. "Maybe," he said softly, "I underrated man's abilities when I said nothing human could have the ferocity in the eyes of that thing we found. I wish we could have the opportunity to treat in a more befitting manner these things. Something with boiling oil, or melted lead in it, or maybe slow roasting in the power boiler. When I think what a man Dutton was—

"Never mind. My theory is confirmed by—by one who knew? Well, Van Wall and Barclay are proven. I think, then, that I'll try to show you what I already know. That I, too, am human." McReady swished the scalpel in absolute alcohol, burned it off the metal blade, and cut the base of his thumb expertly.

Twenty seconds later he looked up from the desk at the waiting men. There were more grins out there now, friendly grins, yet withal, something else in the eyes.

"Connant," McReady laughed softly, "was right. The huskies watching that thing in the corridor bend had nothing on you. Wonder why we think only the wolf blood has the right to ferocity? Maybe on spontaneous viciousness a wolf takes tops, but after these seven days—abandon all hope, ye wolves who enter here!

"Maybe we can save time. Connant, would you step for—"

Again Barclay was too slow. There were more grins, less tensity still, when Barclay and Van Wall finished their work.

Garry spoke in a low, bitter voice. "Connant was one of the finest men we had here—and five minutes ago I'd have sworn he was a man. Those damnable things are more than imitation." Garry shuddered and sat back in his bunk.

And thirty seconds later, Garry's blood shrank from the hot platinum wire, and struggled to escape the tube, struggled as frantically as a suddenly feral, red-eyed, dissolving imitation of Garry struggled to dodge the snake-tongue weapon Barclay advanced at him, white faced and sweating. The Thing in the test-tube screamed with a tiny, tinny voice as McReady dropped it into the glowing coal of the galley stove.

FOURTEEN

"THE LAST OF IT?" Dr. Copper looked down from his bunk with bloodshot, saddened eyes. "Fourteen of them—"

McReady nodded shortly. "In some ways—if only we could have permanently prevented their spreading—I'd like to have even the imitations back. Commander Garry—Connant—Dutton—Clark—"

"Where are they taking those things?" Copper nodded to the stretcher Barclay and Norris were carrying out.

"Outside. Outside on the ice, where they've got fifteen smashed crates, half a ton of coal, and presently will add ten gallons of kerosene. We've dumped acid on every spilled drop, every torn fragment. We're going to incinerate those."

"Sounds like a good plan." Copper nodded wearily.

"I wonder, you haven't said whether Blair—"

McReady started. "We forgot him! We had so much else! I wonder—do you suppose we can cure him now?"

"If—" began Dr. Copper, and stopped meaningly.

McReady started a second time. "Even a madman. It imitated Kinner and his praying hysteria—" McReady turned toward Van Wall at the long table. "Van, we've got to make an expedition to Blair's shack."

Van looked up sharply, the frown of worry faded for an instant in surprised remembrance. Then he rose, nodded. "Barclay better go along. He applied the lashings, and may figure how to get in without frightening Blair too much."

Three quarters of an hour, through –37 cold, while the Aurora curtain bellied overhead. The twilight was nearly 12 hours long, flaming in the north on snow like white, crystalline sand under their skis. A 5-mile wind piled it in drift-lines pointing off to the northwest. Three quarters of an hour to reach the snow-buried shack. No smoke came from the little shack, and the men hastened.

"Blair!" Barclay roared into the wind when he was still a hundred yards away. "Blair!"

"Shut up," said McReady softly. "And hurry. He may be trying a lone hike. If we have to go after him—no planes, the tractors disabled—"

"Would a monster have the stamina a man has?"

"A broken leg wouldn't stop it for more than a minute," McReady pointed out.

Barclay gasped suddenly and pointed aloft. Dim in the twilit sky, a winged thing circled in curves of indescribable grace and ease. Great white wings tipped gently, and the bird swept over them in silent curiosity. "Albatross—" Barclay said softly. "First of the season, and wandering way inland for some reason. If a monster's loose—"

Norris bent down on the ice, and tore hurriedly at his heavy, wind-proof clothing. He straightened, his coat flapping open, a grim blue-metaled weapon in his hand. It roared a challenge to the white silence of Antarctica.

The thing in the air screamed hoarsely. Its great wings worked frantically as a dozen feathers floated down from its tail. Norris fired again. The bird was moving swiftly now, but in an almost straight line of retreat. It screamed again, more feathers dropped and with beating wings it soared behind a ridge of pressure ice, to vanish.

Norris hurried after the others. "It won't come back," he panted.

Barclay cautioned him to silence, pointing. A curiously, fiercely blue light beat out from the cracks of the shack's door. A very low, soft humming sounded inside, a low, soft humming and a clink and clank of tools, the very sounds somehow bearing a message of frantic haste.

McReady's face paled. "Lord help us if that thing has—" He grabbed Barclay's shoulder, and made snipping motions with his fingers, pointing toward the lacing of control-cables that held the door.

Barclay drew the wire-cutters from his pocket, and kneeled soundlessly at the door. The snap and twang of cut wires made an unbearable racket in the utter quiet of the Antarctic hush. There was only that strange, sweetly soft hum from within the shack, and the queerly, hectically clipped clicking and rattling of tools to drown their noises.

McReady peered through a crack in the door. His breath sucked in huskily and his great fingers clamped cruelly on Barclay's shoulder. The meteorologist backed down. "It isn't," he explained very softly, "Blair. It's kneeling on something on the bunk—something that keeps lifting. Whatever it's working on is a thing like a knapsack—and it lifts."

"All at once," Barclay said grimly. "No Norris, hang back, and get that iron of yours out. It may have—weapons."

Together, Barclay's powerful body and McReady's giant strength struck the door. Inside, the bunk jammed against the door screeched madly and crackled into kindling. The door flung down from broken hinges, the patched lumber of the doorpost dropping inward.

Like a blue-rubber ball, a Thing bounced up. One of its four tentacle-like arms looped out like a striking snake. In a seven-tentacled hand a six-inch pencil of winking, shining metal glinted and swung upward to face them. Its line-thin lips twitched back from snake-fangs in a grin of hate, red eyes blazing.

Norris' revolver thundered in the confined space. The hate-washed face twitched in agony, the looping tentacle snatched back. The silvery thing in its hand a smashed ruin of metal, the seven-tentacled hand became a mass of mangled flesh oozing greenish-yellow ichor. The revolver thundered three times more. Dark holes drilled each of the three eyes before Norris hurled the empty weapon against its face.

The thing screamed a feral hate, a lashing tentacle wiping at blinded eyes. For a moment it crawled on the floor, savage tentacles lashing out, the body twitching. Then it staggered up again, blinded eyes working, boiling hideously, the crushed flesh sloughing away in sodden gobbets.

Barclay lurched to his feet and dove forward with an ice-ax. The flat of the weighty thing crushed against the side of the head. Again the unkillable monster went down. The tentacles lashed out, and suddenly Barclay fell to his feet in the grip of a living, livid rope. The thing dissolved as he held it, a white-hot band that ate into the flesh of his hands like living fire. Frantically he tore the stuff from him, held his hands where they could not be reached. The blind Thing felt and ripped at the tough, heavy, windproof cloth, seeking flesh—flesh it could convert—

The huge blowtorch McReady had brought coughed solemnly. Abruptly it rumbled disapproval throatily. Then it laughed gurglingly, and thrust out a blue-white, three-foot tongue. The Thing on the floor shrieked, flailed out blindly with tentacles that writhed and withered in the bubbling wrath of the blowtorch. It crawled and turned on the floor, it shrieked and hobbled madly, but always McReady held the blowtorch on the face, the dead eyes burning and bubbling uselessly. Frantically the Thing crawled and howled.

A tentacle sprouted a savage talon—and crisped in the flame. Steadily McReady moved with a planned, grim campaign. Helpless, maddened, the Thing retreated from the grunting torch, the caressing, licking tongue. For a moment it rebelled, squalling in inhuman hatred at the touch of icy snow. Then it fell back before the charring breath of the torch, the stench of its flesh bathing it. Hopelessly it retreated—on and on across the Antarctic snow, The bitter wind swept over it, twisting the torch-tongue; vainly it flopped, a trail of oily, stinking smoke bubbling away from it—

McReady walked back toward the shack silently. Barclay met him at the door. "No more?" the giant meteorologist asked grimly.

Barclay shook his head. "No more. It didn't split?"

"It had other things to think about," McReady assured him. "When I left it, it was a glowing coal. What was it doing?"

Norris laughed shortly. "Wise boys, we are. Smash magnetos, so planes won't work. Rip the boiler tubing out of the tractors. And leave that Thing alone for a week in this shack. Alone and undisturbed."

McReady looked in at the shack more carefully. The air, despite the ripped door, was hot and humid. On a table at the far end of the room rested a thing of coiled wires and small magnets, glass tubing and radio tubes. At the center a block of rough stone rested. From the center of the block came the light that flooded the place, the fiercely blue light bluer than the glare of an electric arc, and from it came the sweetly soft hum. Off to one side was another mechanism of crystal glass, blown with an incredible neatness and delicacy, metal plates and a queer, shimmery sphere of insubstantiality.

"What is that?" McReady moved nearer.

Norris grunted. "Leave it for investigation. But I can guess pretty well. That's atomic power. That stuff to the left—that's a neat little thing for doing what men have been trying to do with hundred-ton cyclotrons and so forth. It separates neutrons from heavy water, which he was getting from the surrounding ice."

"Where did he get all—oh. Of course, A monster couldn't be locked in—or out. He's been through the apparatus caches." McReady stared at the apparatus. "Lord, what minds that race must have—"

"The shimmery sphere—I think it's a sphere of pure force. Neutrons can pass through any matter, and he wanted a supply reservoir of neutrons. Just project neutrons against silica—calcium—beryllium—almost anything, and the atomic energy is released. That thing is the atomic generator."

McReady plucked a thermometer from his coat. "It's 120° in here, despite the open door. Our clothes have kept the heat out to an extent, but I'm sweating now."

Norris nodded. "The light's cold. I found that. But

it gives off heat to warm the place through that coil. He had all the power in the world. He could keep it warm and pleasant, as his race thought of warmth and pleasantness. Did you notice the light, the color of it?"

McReady nodded. "Beyond the stars is the answer. From beyond the stars. From a hotter planet that circled a brighter, bluer sun they came."

McReady glanced out the door toward the blasted, smoke-stained trail that flopped and wandered blindly off across the drift. "There won't be any more coming, I guess. Sheer accident it landed here, and that was twenty million years ago. What did it do all that for?" he nodded toward the apparatus.

Barclay laughed softly. "Did you notice what it was working on when we came? Look." He pointed toward the ceiling of the shack.

Like a knapsnack made of flattened coffee tins, with dangling cloth straps and leather belts, the mechanism clung to the ceiling. A tiny, glaring heart of supernal flame burned in it, yet burned through the ceiling's wood without scorching it. Barclay walked over to it, grasped two of the dangling straps in his hands, and pulled it down with an effort. He strapped it about his body. A slight jump carried him in a weirdly slow arc across the room.

"Anti-gravity," said McReady softly.

"Anti-gravity," Norris nodded. "Yes, we had 'em stopped, with no planes, and no birds. The birds hadn't come—but they had coffee tins and radio parts, and glass and the machine shop at night.

And a week—a whole week—all to itself. America in a single jump—with anti-gravity powered by the atomic energy of matter.

"We had 'em stopped. Another half hour—it was just tightening these straps on the device so it could wear it—and we'd have stayed in Antarctica, and shot down any moving thing that came from, the rest of the world."

"The albatross—" McReady said softly. "Do you suppose—"

"With this thing almost finished? With that death weapon it held in its hand?

"No, by the grace of God, who evidently does hear very well, even down here, and the margin of half an hour, we keep our world, and the planets of the system, too. Anti-gravity, you know, and atomic power. Because They came from another sun, a star beyond the stars. *They* came from a world with a bluer sun."

WHO GOES THERE?

the
screen treatment

by William F. Nolan

based on the story by **john w. campbell**

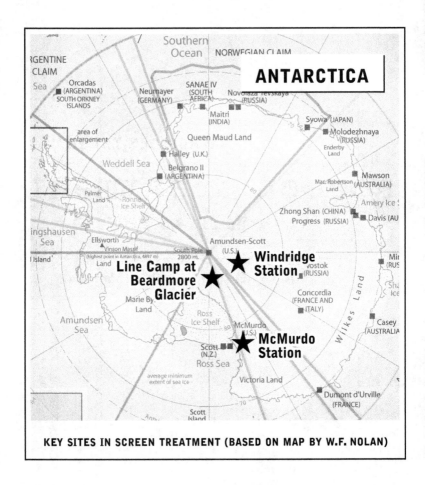

KEY SITES IN SCREEN TREATMENT (BASED ON MAP BY W.F. NOLAN)

WHO GOES THERE?

(Screen Treatment)

by

William F. Nolan

We open in Polar twilight—the surreal, other-worldy twilight of Antarctica, the immense frozen continent of snow-capped bergs, endless ice fields and thrusting glacial cliffs. We are on the vast ice plain between the South Pole and Beardmore Glacier, watching several parka-clad members of a team, as they engage in what seems to be some type of intense field activity. We discover they are playing baseball, as a solidly hit homer ends the game. (In their bulky clothing, which restricts movement, the players are quite awkward—and the sport takes on the character of comic opera.)

As we enter Windridge (a complex, fully equipped, below-ice scientific station) we discover that the batter who hit the home run is a woman, MARGE POMROY. She's in her 30s, a meteorologist—the wife of RALPH POMROY (whose specialty is glacial science, or core-sampling). At the moment, her husband and two other scientists are working the ice beyond Windridge, at a field camp some miles distant.

Marge begins preparing one of her helium-filled weather balloons for a tracking launch—checking with radioman MIKE GONZALES regarding her husband. Mike tells her that Pomroy and the others are due to break camp soon for their return to the ice station. "But they want to use the light as long as possible." (It is important to understand that life at the South Pole is geared to long, unbroken periods of light and darkness—six months of each. As our film begins, the sun is below the horizon and the twilight period is almost over. Soon the Polar night will close in on Windridge.)

In all, representing several Stateside universities, there are nine men and three women assigned to Windridge Station, each with a specific job. Every station in Antarctica has a "scientific leader"—and here the man is "MAC" MACREADY, a space physicist from

UCLA. In his early 30s, a quirky, rebellious individual with a questing mind who is at Windridge to study that spectacular atmospheric phenomenon known as the Aurora.

He is into a relationship with LIZBETH BEN-NETT, late 20s, also from Southern California (Cal Tech) who "doubles" between working the data computers and tending her hydroponic "greenhouse" at the station. Macready and Liz lived together in L.A. before this Antarctic sojourn—but discreetly maintain separate quarters at Windridge. Liz is a dedicated scientist, and keeps to a busy schedule.

Another female scientist handles seismology (Earth Studies) at Windridge. She is CARLA RALSEN, the youngest of the three women stationed there. Carla is almost neurotically possessive regarding the delicate seismometer she has set up at the end of a long tunnel outside the compound; no one is allowed near it without her say so.

She is close to and confides with Marge Pomroy (theirs is a pseudo-daughter/mother relationship). Because of this, Carla has a problem with VINCE STOD-DARD, who wants to marry her. Vince is disturbed by

Carla's dependence on the older woman.

Stoddard is part of the civilian (non-scientist) "support group" at the station. He's a utility expert (who takes care of the water supply, which must be melted down and processed from the ice). Grew up in New York. He came to Antarctica with his buddy, TED STEINMETZ, a mechanic, electrician (in charge of the vital power generators).

Steinmetz is the most unstable member of the group, prone to over-drinking and temper flare-ups. There's a lot of "dead time" during these long months on the ice and Ted hates it here; he's sorry he signed on at Windridge and is already grousing about the fast-approaching winter (which will leave them cut off from all outside contact for half a year).

Medical treatment at the station is in the hands of DR. RICHARD BLAIR, the team's official "father figure," a man in his early 50s, who maintains a leavening sense of humor. (He's interested in penguin psychology, viewing the birds, however, with a mixture of wariness and distaste. "Cute, hell! They'll have at you with flipper and beak!")

WINNIE NORRIS, the cook, completes the support group. He's a rail-thin, sad-eyed man who never seems to enjoy any of the food he serves. He's in the Polar wilderness to escape the legal and emotional problems of three ex-wives and five kids—and looks upon women as "the enemy."

The three men (which we have yet to meet in the film) camped in tents beyond the station itself are RALPH POMROY, FRANK KELLY and DAVE BANNING. Ralph and Frank are veterans (they've "wintered over" here before), while Dave, their young associate, working for his doctorate in Glaciology, is new to the ice.

There's one more member of the Windridge team: the station mascot. He's a mixed blood (Husky/ Malemute) pup named MACHO—whose first birthday creates celebration that day. The happily spoiled animal is a target of much playful rough-housing. No doubt of it: Macho is convinced he's human.

During the opening section of the film we establish the reality of our characters through their routine of work-and-recreation in this rugged, isolated terrain at the South Polar Cap:

We are with Macready as he checks computer

data with Liz on his latest sky photos...we follow Carla Ralsen along her special ice tunnel as she takes an earth reading from her seismometer...we play a brief bit with Steinmetz as he struggles to repair a faulty generator part...we are with Marge Pomroy at the launch of a helium balloon from the weather tower.

This balloon becomes a "linking" device, as CAMERA tracks it into the sky, PANNING to show us a swiftly moving metallic object. And, at this point, we switch inside the craft—to an overflight view of the Antarctic shelf, via distorted-lens EFFECT (which we later realize is the POINT OF VIEW of the alien beings, this lens effect representing the way they see our world).

The flyover, which includes a full sweep of Windridge Station, carries us beyond the area on out to the thrusting peaks of the Beardmore Glacier range, where the alien POINT OF VIEW shows us a 3-man field camp, pitched close to the glacier itself.

The camp consists of a trio of reinforced red nylon tents staked to the ice. A motorized "Snowcat" is parked nearby, with an empty pack-sled behind it. Boxes of equipment are stacked around the tents.

Now we are down on the ice with Pomroy, Kelly and Banning—as they drill through the frozen surface to extract a core sample. In the cold twilight the work is rough and exhausting....

The three men are startled to see a dark, glinting shape pass swiftly over them—to drop from sight beyond the glacier's far edge. Possibly a meteor; if so, a really big one! And why no sound of impact? "Let's check it out," says Pomroy.

Banning radios to Mike Gonzales at Windridge, telling him what they saw and that they are going to investigate. He provides Mike with the area coordinates.

Then we see them roar off in the Snowcat.

INTERCUT to a brief scene at dinner back in the station: Macho's birthday party. All of the Windridge team are gathered for this festive sequence (allowing individual character traits to emerge). In these INTER-CUTS we share Blair's easy humor, Ted's drinking, the cook's melancholy, etc.

At Beardmore, the Snowcat stops and the three dismount, setting out for the cliff. Pomroy is certain that the object dropped into this area. They round an angled section of rock to confront: an alien spacecraft, dark and silent, made of smooth black metal and shaped like the head of a spear. (It is a scout ship, only large enough to hold a crew of three.)

Shock and awe soon give way to curiosity. Is anyone (or anything) alive inside? There is absolutely no sound or movement from the craft—but a circular section of hull gapes open.

Cautiously, the three move forward...entering the craft.

And, as they do, the hull seals itself silently behind them.

DISSOLVE TO: Windridge—some time later—as the trio of Pomroy, Banning and Kelly returns in the Snowcat, their pack-sled loaded with gear and core samples. They seem perfectly normal—tired, but satisfied with their field work, glad to be back.

Macready asks them what they found near the cliff. Not a thing. He, of all people, knows how the Antarctic sky can play visual tricks; the "sighting" was an optical illusion. Mac accepts their story.

But we see Macho, standing rigidly to one side,

staring at the three men. There's an <u>intense</u> interest in his animal eyes....

While the Polar twilight deepens, moving toward seasonal darkness, the members of Windridge chart their own windowless, below-ice "days" and "nights." During each "night period" the lights are dimmed in all of the work tunnels to save valuable energy—and there is near-total darkness in the sleeping area.

In their separately partitioned room (on the night following Ralph's return from the ice) Marge Pomroy wakes from sleep, gasping and terrified. Ralph attempts to comfort her as she tells him of her horribly real nightmare in which he was her "enemy." "In my dream," she says, "you tried to <u>kill me</u>!"

CUT TO: next morning. Dr. Blair consults with Marge. He tells her that such a nightmare is not unusual: loved ones often assume reverse roles in dreams, as our minds deal with stored tensions. She needn't feel guilty.

But we, the audience, know that her dream was an all-too-real mental warning—for now Ralph Pomroy <u>is</u> the enemy, along with Carl Banning and Frank Kel-

ly—although the three men <u>seem</u> their normal selves,
working over their core samples in the station lab that
afternoon.

Mac is puzzled by the fact that frisky, friendly Macho refuses to enter the lab where Pomroy and
the others are working. "You guys spill anything in
here? Maybe Macho smells something we don't." They
shrug; everything's fine. Mac considers it odd, but
drops the subject....

That night the CAMERA shows us the <u>empty</u>
bunks of Banning and Kelly—then takes us to Ralph
Pomroy, lying beside his wife in their room, eyes staring. He does not blink, just stares—as Marge moans in
her sleep, victim to another disturbing dream.

Morning—as Winnie Norris prepares food for
the station breakfast. Up to now, Macho has always
haunted the kitchen for scraps whenever Norris prepares a meal—but the dog is not around this morning.
And no one's seen him.

We CUT from the cook's puzzlement at Macho's
disappearance to a sequence on the ice, wherein Vince

Stoddard has taken one of the smaller and faster Snow-cats out to retrieve one of Marge Pomroy's weather balloons. Ted Steinmetz is with him, complaining about how bored his is at the prospect of being "marooned" out here at the Pole "for six lousy months"...(He's nursing a hangover from the previous night's drinking.)

Directed by short-wave radio, they find the balloon (homing in on its signal)—but they also find:

The frozen body of Macho.

CUT TO: Mac, asking Dr. Blair: "But how did he die? What killed him?" Blair can give no answer to this. There's not a mark of any kind on the animal's body—and no poisoned food was found in his stomach.

Mac recalls that the dog has been acting strangely; maybe Macho's odd actions and his sudden death are linked in some way....

Carla Ralsen has a sequence with Marge. The younger girl is concerned with the fact that Marge is still having the same kind of dream—in which she's threatened by her husband. Worried about her friend, Carla insists that Dr. Blair administer a sedative; pills have not helped. He gives Marge a shot that evening—to help her sleep soundly. He, too, is concerned with these abnormal nightmares....

Now we are watching Mac, as he photographs the incredible Aurora from the domed station observatory. Liz Bennett is with him—and she considers the colorful sky display equally fascinating. As Mac takes his pictures he talks about the change in Marge Pomroy, how "down" she's been. Women are still rare at the South Pole, and the tensions and the isolation may exact a heavier toll on them. Nonsense, says Liz. Something else is responsible for Marge Pomroy's dreams....

Later: Carla Ralsen brings Mac a very unusual report. Her current readings have revealed some type of sporadic seismic activity beneath the station. In the ice cap itself. Mac is surprised. "But we've never had a quake recorded in this area." Could it be an error? No, her force-wave readings clearly indicate a disturbance below the ice. She'll keep checking....

That night, with the tunnels dimmed and the sleep areas shrouded in darkness, Marge Pomroy lies in drugged slumber next to her husband. Ralph is awake, standing beside the bed, his eyes intense as the door to their room opens. Banning and Kelly are there. All three stare down at the sleeping woman. Then Ralph takes her strongly into his arms—and a horrifying change begins; from the fingers of his hands, from his open mouth, from his eyes, glowing strands of yellow emerge, like tendrils of living fire, to penetrate the pores of the woman's body. And, as his alien self pours into the living body of Marge Pomroy, the body of Ralph Pomroy begins to wither and die. He slowly folds down, into himself, as if he is a sack being emptied of all inner matter....

Morning: In the station's medical lab. Marge is there, bright and smiling, telling Dr. Blair how soundly she slept and how well she feels. "I'm sure the nightmares are over," she tells Blair. He nods, "I hope you're right." She smiles. "I know I am."

But when Carla attempts to talk to Marge about her odd seismic readings the older woman puts her off, moves away to other duties. There is a "coldness" separating them.

Mac is trying to locate Ralph Pomroy, but Ralph is not at the station. With Steinmetz, he checks the garage area—to find a Snowcat missing. Why would Pomroy leave so abruptly, telling no one?

"That's not true," says Marge, appearing in the doorway. "Ralph told me." He left during the night hours, she explains, to bring back a piece of equipment needed to complete his core experiments. "He did not want to wake anyone. Its as simple as that."

But Mac is not satisfied. He goes to the radio room, instructs Mike Gonzales to contact McMurdo station. He wants to talk to Pomroy as soon as he reaches the station.

But Mike is unable to comply with Mac's order. The radio is <u>dead</u>. No way to send or receive messages until he can locate the mechanical trouble. How long will it take? No way of telling. "Entire rig has to be checked, every part." This breakdown has Gonzales stymied; he just can't figure the cause. He does tell Mac that the last incoming message he got indicated that some blizzard weather was moving in....

Mac continues with his station duties, working with Liz at the computer on Aurora data analysis—but he's concerned by Pomroy's sudden leave-taking.

A small 2-man copter is garaged at Windridge, usually piloted by Carl Banning. Now the craft is being readied for takeoff. Banning tells Mac that since the bad weather (and the fast-approaching darkness) will soon make flying impossible he wants to take a final run out to Beardmore for a special deep-ice core sample.

"I'll take Stoddard with me to co-pilot," he says.

Mac okays the flight—and the copter takes off that same afternoon with Banning and Vince Stoddard aboard.

But the moment they are airborne Banning goes silent, making no reply to Stoddard's comments. His manner is suddenly cold and remote. We go in, very close, on Banning's eyes. They glow with yellow light....

Next: a brief follow-up scene at the glacier—as the "new" Vince Stoddard emerges from the copter, carrying the deflated, sack-like body of Carl Banning. He moves to the black, silent scout craft, still nestled under the cliff, places Banning's corpse inside the ship, steps away—aims a tube-shaped laser device at the spacecraft. A powerful laser beam blasts the ship to black ash against the rocks.

Back at Windridge, the copter sets down with Stoddard at the controls. "Where the hell's Banning?" Mac wants to know. Stoddard says that Carl "took sick" and that he dropped him off for treatment at McMurdo. "Appendix attack for sure. I knew Blair couldn't handle it." Says he talked to Pomroy there, and Ralph will be staying on with Banning until the recovery.

Mac has no choice but to accept this explanation. With the radio still out he can't verify with McMurdo.

That night—as the others sleep—we follow Stoddard, Kelly and Marge Pomroy as they move silently down the dim ice tunnels toward the hydroponics shack. They do not speak to one another; verbal communication is not necessary between them.

Inside the menacing gloom of the greenhouse they remove some boards in the flooring—to reveal a tunnel, leading downward. As they enter, we see that each of the three carries a tube-thin laser device (the same type we saw used at the glacier). The lasers sizzle into glowing life as they begin using the cutting beams to widen and deepen the tunnel. They cut their way downward.

Later that same night: we are with Winnie Norris as he moves along one of the tunnels leading to the greenhouse. Winnie is after some kitchen supplies, and the food he seeks is stored in this tunnel. He selects a box, and is in the process of removing several frozen steaks when he notices an odd flicker of illumination deep in the ice beneath the tunnel floor...like a series of moving lights in dense fog.

These lights lead him toward the greenhouse—which he enters. More deep-ice illumination near the far corner of the building. Winnie crosses to the area, notes a bit of loose flooring. Uncovers the mouth of the tunnel, takes a flash from a shelf—and starts downward.

But he does not get far. Three shapes materialize from the gloom: Stoddard, Marge and Kelly. Silent. Unsmiling. All staring at him with unblinking eyes.

Norris speaks to them, asks what they're doing here? What kind of tunnel is this? No reply. Kelly moves toward him, and Winnie is suddenly fearful; he steps back, reaching for the cleaver at his belt. (We have established that he carried this meat cleaver in a belt sling, using it to cut the frozen steaks.) Now he panics, buries the blade in the neck of Frank Kelly.

Incredibly—no blood! Instead, a glowing tendril of energized light pools out from the "wound," toward Winnie Norris, whose back is to the tunnel wall. More gleaming threads of energized matter flow out from Kelly's host-body to envelop the cook—until the drained, wrinkled corpse of Frank Kelly folds to the iced floor in a loose spill of boneless flesh....

Next morning: Mac is in the photolab, developing his latest batch of atmosphere shots when Liz comes in to tell him that Kelly is missing. She'd gone looking for him, with some computer data he needed, and: "He's gone...nowhere in the station. Finally, we checked the garage and another Snowcat's gone. Then we found this note in his bunk. Addressed to you."

The note reads: "Can't take the thought of being holed up here all winter. So I'm joining the others at McMurdo. Sorry!" It is signed, "Frank."

Macready is totally shaken by this, and tells Liz he is now convinced that the truth is not being told in regard to all the recent disappearances. First, Pomroy takes off without informing him; then Banning is hit with an appendix attack; now it's Frank Kelly who—

Mac hesitates. "<u>Pomroy</u>...<u>Banning</u>...<u>Kelly</u>! They were together at Beardmore, checking on the meteor—"

"But they didn't find anything," declares Liz.

"Maybe not—but I've got the coordinates...and I'm going to have a look for myself."

CUT TO: Mac, airborne over the Beardmore range in the station's copter. The weather is much rougher; he's fighting crosswinds—but, as he checks a map during a pass over the area, he sees something near the inner cliff.

Mac lands the copter—reaches the exact spot where the alien scout ship landed. Now there is only a charred blackness burned into the rock face—all that remains of the ship. No, not <u>quite</u> all—as we see Mac sift through the ashes, to come up with a small, twisted bit of fire-blackened metal....

We are back at the lab in Windridge, where Mac is finishing a test on the metal fragment. Liz and Dr. Blair are with him, and he tells them that he cannot identify the fragment as any known Earth metal.

Still, he's not an expert in this field...Question is: what <u>could</u> it be a piece of? Blair suggests that it could be from a new Soviet test vehicle which crashed and burned there.

"One thing's for sure," says Mac. "<u>Something</u> damned strange landed near that cliff...."

A meeting is called. Full group: Mac, Liz, Carla, Dr. Blair, Marge, Winnie Norris, Stoddard, Gonzales and Ted Steinmetz. Mac tells them that he believes Pomroy, Banning and Kelly lied about finding nothing at the glacier. "Some type of vehicle crashed there. I found part of it." And he holds up the fragment.

So, asks Stoddard, what does it <u>mean</u>? Why would the three lie about what they'd found? Mac doesn't know—but he thinks it ties in, somehow, with the death of Macho, the radio blackout, and the sudden departures of Pomroy and Kelly. What is Mac leading up to?

A vote, says Macready. Bad weather is due, and they're running out of flying time. He feels that it would be wise to strike the camp and head for McMurdo. Three round trips in the copter could handle all nine of them. He calls for a vote on this.

"We still have a job to do here," says Vince Stoddard. "Nothing you've said has changed my mind about staying."

But Steinmetz votes to get out now. He thinks Kelly was smart to split when he did. A heated discussion becomes all but explosive, but the station's "team spirit" holds. The vote. 3 to go, 6 to stay.

"Okay," sighs Mac. "We stay."

Now they become truly isolated—as the six-month polar night closes over Windridge Station, accompanied by howling winds and blizzard conditions.

Despite this, the scientific work continues—as Dr. Blair reminds Macready that there is no real proof of anything being seriously amiss—and that once Gonzales gets the radio repaired they can contact McMurdo and verify the fact that Kelly and Pomroy and Banning are there.

"We won't be talking to McMurdo," Mac says darkly. "Mike's gone over every inch of his equipment."

The radioman has found no fault in his rig—yet the radio remains totally dead.

That night Carla Ralsen goes to Marge, confessing that she's frightened and confused. Marge <u>must</u> listen to her. (And the older woman does seem willing to do so.) Carla says that she's been getting stronger below-ice reading—and she feels that the disturbance below the station is <u>not</u> a natural one; someone is <u>causing</u> it. Has she told Mac? No, only about the readings, not about her suspicions. Marge advises her to talk to Vince Stoddard; Vince loves her, has been worried about her.

Carla agrees to see Vince. As she leaves Winnie Norris, walks from the shadow to stand beside Marge. Their eyes burn in the darkness....

Carla enters the garage at the far end of the station, and Vince is there, tinkering with the engine of a snow tractor. The looming bulk of machinery lends an aura of tension to the scene....

Carla's glad to see him. Why has he been <u>avoiding</u> her of late? "Oh, but I haven't. Not really," says Stoddard—and takes her into his arms. We, as well as Carla, see his eyes begin to fill with flickering yellow fire. Shocked and terrified, she backs away, runs to the exit. But Stoddard has locked the garage door; she cannot reach the tunnel.

In panic, she lunges away—onto the control seat of the heavy snow tractor Vince has been working on. Its engine is still running. She guns it, aiming the machine for Stoddard, using the massive metal-nose plow to pin him against the wall. But, horribly, Stoddard smiles—as his host-body is crushed by the plow-blade. Obviously, he does not feel any pain—and, again, there is no blood! Snake tendrils of yellow dart from his mouth, eyes, hands...emerging from his collapsing corpse to encircle Carla....

Later: an energy failure—as the lights in the station dim...go out, then back on....

We see Steinmetz in the power room, working on the main generator. He swears, throws down his tools, and reports to Mac. Problem: the generator is losing power, and he can't figure why. If the power loss continues, they can switch to the backup generator, but even the backup won't last long if the condition persists. And if that one goes..."It's your job to make sure it doesn't!" snaps Mac.

And he seeks out Carla, asks to see her latest seismic report. Looks it over. "There's no indication here of below-ice activity," he says. She tells him that her original readings were off. No disturbance below Windridge. She made a mistake. "Everything's normal," she asserts.

No, Mac insists, things are far from normal. He stares hard at her. "And I don't know why—but I think you're lying to me."

The temperature inside the station continues to drop. As the lights go dim, heavy clothing is now worn, even during sleep periods. Mac has made a decision: the storm is clearning, and he will authorize use of the copter to evacuate the station via round trips to McMurdo. No more voting; the generator problem has eliminated choice.

Steinmetz asks for one more try at the generators. Okay, but if he can't fix 'em, the fly-outs begin tomorrow.

That night Liz jarred from sleep. She sits up in bed, awakened by a sound in the greenhouse. A thudding noise. She gets up, opens her door, moves into the narrow tunnelway leading to the hydroponics shack. Light, faint but distinct, flickers under the edge of the door....

When she gets there the light is gone. Sudden silence. No sound or light from within.

Liz pushes the door open...There is a dim, smokey illumination framing the profusion of plants and flowers (many of which are withering from the increasing cold).

"Anyone in here?" Her voice is edged with tension. No reply. She moves down the gloomed lane between the heavy green plants, walking slowly. Liz reaches the end of the row and, with a shock, realizes that someone is standing very close to her in the semi-darkness. Dr. Blair.

She gasps, draws back. "What...I...I woke up...a sound...something falling...."

Blair regards her with placid eyes, smiles faintly. "One of your plants. I knocked it over."

And we see the smashed pot scattered along the board flooring.

"Is...anyone here with you?"

No, Dr. Blair tells her, he is quite alone.

"But...alone...this time of night?"

To meditate, he says, while the others sleep. He comes here often. Now he excuses himself, telling her he's sorry about the plant.

But after he leaves, Liz stares down at the flooring; something had caught her eye. CAMERA PANS to a tall, wooden storage locker. Its door is slightly ajar, and the edge of a <u>woman's shoe</u> is visible.

Very slowly, Liz pulls open the locker—then gasps in shock and revulsion.

Stuffed into the locker: the boneless, sucked-dry corpse of Marge Pomroy.

We are into a scene in the medical lab, involving Mac, Liz and Dr. Blair...The doctor has finished his examination, and the remains of Marge Pomroy lie under a sheet on the lab table.

Blair admits he's never seen anything like it... muscles and interior organs gone, most of the bones "dissolved." But he attempts to render a medical explanation:

"An incredibly fast-growing form of cancerous growth—acting with terrible speed on all of the body cells...triggered, perhaps, by the unique conditions here at the Pole."

"Shouldn't we warn the others?" asks Liz.

"Of what?" says Blair. "We don't know if this thing is contagious—or how to fight it if it is!"

He advises against telling anyone else—until he can spend time studying the body, to determine more about the disease. No one is to enter the med lab until he gives his permission.

In the mess hall, over hot coffee, Mac tells Liz that he thinks the same thing that happened to Marge happened to Pomroy, Banning and Kelly. If so, asks Liz, where are the bodies?

"Probably destroyed. By Blair. He didn't have time to get rid of Marge before you came into the greenhouse."

She's shocked; is he accusing Dr. Blair?

"I'm saying he lied to us. Carla's also involved. And I don't know who else?"

"Involved in what?"

"It has something to do with what landed near the glacier...with Macho's death...with seismic activity below the camp...the radio and generators failing... They're all tied into it."

The point is, he tells her, they must not trust anyone. Not Blair or Carla, Steinmetz or any others. "Whatever's happened has <u>affected</u> some of them—maybe all of them."

Then what's to be done; how do they <u>prove</u> any of this?

"We start by finding out what's going on below the ice," says Mac. "Carla lied about those readings..."

They'll start at the greenhouse: "I want to know why Blair was in there!"

They are moving down one of the narrow passageways when Steinmetz and Gonzales appear at a fork in the tunnel. At this point neither Mac nor Liz (or we, the audience) is sure who's a friend and who's an enemy.

The four confront one another in the dimming, frosted corridor. Then Steinmetz says: "Mike and I have been working on the generator. No use. Power's almost gone. We were heading for the radio shack—to have another go at the rig."

"Yeah," nods Gonzales. "Got to reach McMurdo. Let 'em know our situation."

Liz starts to speak, but Mac stops her. (She's to trust <u>nobody</u>.) "Okay," he says. "Give it another try. But we'll be flying out of here in any case."

They continue along the tunnel as we follow Gonzales and Steinmetz into the radio room. CAMERA IN on the eyes of Mike Gonzales as they begin to glow.

He moves toward Steinmetz....

Inside the greenhouse Mac is carefully checking the floor around the locker....

CUT TO: Blair and Carla—as they enter the radio shack, to face the "new" Ted Steinmetz. The drained corpse of Mike Gonzales lies crumpled in one corner.

The three aliens leave silently, heading down the corridor—toward the greenhouse.

Inside, Mac has just uncovered the entrance to the ice tunnel. We see him check the clip on a .45, then enter the tunnel with Liz. Behind them, they push the boards carefully back into place to hide the fact of their discovery. Then they start down the tunnel, Mac (with a flash) leading....

Back to the aliens—as Carla, Blair and Steinmetz enter the greenhouse, move to the ice tunnel,
remove the loose flooring, and enter. They move with
unhurried calm.

To Mac and Liz—as they reach the tunnel's end.
There's a glow, a humming of vast, stored energies, just
ahead of them....

Now they emerge into a vast cavern which ex-
tends for miles under the ice—to encounter a stunning
sight: a giant spacecraft fills the cavern, a multi-level
mammoth of tiers and decks and oddly-angled sec-
tions—a star king built to range far galaxies. (Note:
this ship is truly immense—as large as the Empire State
Building placed sideways under the ice!)

The metal skin of the ship glows and pulses,
filling the cavern with intense light....

The total effect is mind-numbing.

Mac and Liz now stand beside the craft, staring
up at it with awe. Finally, Mac says softly: "So this is
what they came for!"

"They?"

"Whoever or whatever they are...aliens from

another solar system...they landed near the glacier... took over Pomroy and the others—then sent them back to gain control of the rest of us...used us."

"Marge," breathes Liz. "But why?"

"They were obviously sent to bring this back." He looks up at the ship. "God knows how many tens of thousands of years it's been buried here under the ice cap...but they cut their way down to it—to bring it back to life."

"Which explains why the generator failed. They were using our power...."

"Yes...to activate the ship's primary drive," says Mac. "Once this thing is fully operational the atomic heat generated by a ship this size at takeoff could melt enough of the polar ice cap to destroy McMurdo Station and everyone in it!"

"But there's no way we can stop it!"

"We've got to try," says Mac.

They range quickly along the side of the mammoth craft, searching for a possible way inside. But the glowing metal is smooth and seamless.

A sound of coming footsteps! Mac grabs Liz and they duck behind a projecting ledge of ice.

Blair, Carla and Steinmetz appear, moving from the tunnel toward the forward hull.

They stop near the ledge—and Blair removes a beam device from his jacket, aims it at the ship. A ground level section of the hull sinks inward.

Blair and the other two aliens enter the space-craft—and just before the hull reseals itself, Mac and Liz are able to slip inside.

The interior is mind bending. Warily, keeping well back, they follow the three aliens upward (via a series of moving ramps) past multi-level crew areas— to the main control deck.

Blair, Steinmetz and Carla step forward—to a wall of curving metal, where they "rack" their tube-shaped laser devices. Then all three move into a circular area embracing the ship's central control unit.

As Liz and Mac watch from the shadows, they see Blair pass his hand over a control stud—and a "shielding" begins to shape itself (from particles of shining matter). It solidifies into a dome which totally covers the circular area.

Now, a glowing, golden mist rises from vents in the flooring to fill the bubble and, as this occurs, we see the aliens shedding their earthbodies as a snake sheds its skin.

Mac and Liz squint their eyes against the blazing, incandescent beings now standing within the bubble. In "natural" form, each creature seems to exist in its own separate core of dazzling light—and through this rippling curtain of brightness we sense the shape, the bones and incredible body structure, of things truly alien...other-worldly.

A hive-hum of sound begins to build within the ship.

"They're getting set to lift off!" says Mac.

"...and take us with them!" murmurs Liz.

Macready breaks from the shadows, runs forward to the dome-bubble's edge, the big .45 gripped in his right fist. (In this sleek, futuristic surrounding, the gun seems an antique—almost ridiculous!)

A metallic voice rings out in warning as Mac points his weapon at the bubble. (Note: This voice forms words in English, but the spacing and pronunciation are alien—and triple-toned—as all three creatures speak with one voice.)

"Be warned, Macready! This craft is about

to depart your planet. Leave at once—or you will not survive."

"You speak of survival—when you've murdered Dr. Blair and all the others...."

"We do not murder," the voice declares. "Of necessity, we utilize native host bodies in order to perform our duties. We use these bodies for food, shelter and disguise—as we do whenever we are assigned to a new planet."

"If you engage full power to lift this ship, you'll kill hundreds more!"

"Their deaths cannot be avoided," says the voice. "This spacecraft, lost here on your Earth, must be returned to our people. We have been sent to reclaim it." Then, a command: "Leave. Now!"

"I'm not leaving—and neither are you!" And Mac fires the .45 at the bubble.

The bullets have no effect.

The rising hum of atomic power is intensified. The ship trembles with energy....

Liz turns past Mac to the curving metal wall, to the racked lasers; she pulls one free, swings toward the bubble, fires.

The laser charge slices through the side of the dome, releasing the life-sustaining atmospheric vapor inside the bubble.

"Now we shall all die," the triple-toned voice coldly declares. "In destroying this shielding you have activated the ship's self-destruct mechanism...."

The hum fades, and a new siren-like sound replaces it. Inside the fractured dome the aliens are weakening, their bodies darkening, shrinking, as the light dies in each of them.

Intent on escape, Mac and Liz run for the exit—the great ship has sealed itself—and they must use lasers to cut their way free.

Now we INTERCUT between their flight for life and the dying spacecraft's instrumentation—as the dials tick and whir toward Self-Destruct. The numerals on the control panel are alien, but the pattern is clear as they record the final minutes until implosion.

Liz and Mac leave the cavern, sprint up the angled ice tunnel toward station level. "At McMurdo..." gasps Liz. "Do they have a chance?"

"I hope so," says Mac. "When this thing

goes Windridge will go with it—but the ice cap might hold...."

We play the final scenes at full tempo, INTER-CUTTING between our protagonists and the clicking instruments on the ship.

Mac reaches the garage, and, with the help of Liz, rolls the station helicopter into the outside darkness. The wind is strong, but the blizzard has passed... Flying is possible.

But will the copter start? "The engine has its own independent heat generator...battery powered. It should kick over!"

And, after several tense moments, it does! The copter blades begin to revolve lazily as Mac pulls the hatch closed. He increases power, throttles for liftoff....

"What about the fuel?" asks Liz.

"Enough to reach McMurdo—if we can get this thing in the air before the ship blows!"

CUT TO: the spacecraft—as the needles merge.

Destruct!

A giant fireball of raw heat ruptures the ice—as

Windridge is blown into fiery ruin.

   The copter <u>is</u> airborne—but the massive shock wave smashes it sideways, as Mac fights for control. A landing skid <u>bangs</u> the ice—but Mac throttles skyward again....

   And they survive. As does McMurdo station—since the explosion was not great enough to destroy the mile-deep ice cap....

   Below, in the final SHOT of our film, only a wide, smoking crater in the polar shelf remains to mark the death of a great starship.

THE END

About William F. Nolan

Critically acclaimed as the author of the iconic SF classic, *Logan's Run* (bestseller, MGM film, CBS television series, etc.), William F. Nolan's prolific career spans more than half a century. He has garnered major awards in each of his primary fields: science fiction (voted Author Emeritus by the SF Writer's of America), dark fantasy (named a living legend by the International Horror Guild), and crime fiction (twice winner of the Edgar Allen Poe Special Award by the Mystery Writer's of America).

William Nolan has 80-plus books to his credit in a variety of global editions, and his work has been selected for some 325 anthologies and textbooks.

He lives and works in Vancouver, Washington, near the Oregon border.

LISTEN UP!

Who Goes There? is also available in **CD audio!** Masterfully narrated, this dramatic presentation brings Campbell's classic to life as never before.

(2.75 Hours, Unabridged, on 2 Compact Discs) Available now at RocketRideBooks.com

Listen to **Masters of SciFi and Horror,** available at RocketRideBooks.com or by free subscription in iTunes.

FICTION SPEAKS DEEPLY to the human condition, even if the issues into which it delves wear the mask of the martian or monster. Science fiction and horror challenge our imagination while causing us to confront our deepest fears. We discuss the acclaimed stories of these genres and the creators behind them.

CPSIA information can be obtained
at www.ICGtesting.com
Printed in the USA
BVHW041159071021
618412BV00004B/93